TRAPPED IN THE FLAMES

In the inferno's light, among the lurching shadows, Clay saw another form stretched on the ground—and this time it *was* the boy, lying on his face. Clay flipped him over, scooped him in his arms, and straightened. His lungs were on fire now and his stinging eyes all but sealed shut. *The door's back that way,* he thought. *Straight back* . . . If he were wrong, he knew there would be no second guess—not with his temples throbbing and his face feeling like an overripe tomato about to burst in the sun. Clay spun and took a first step, when *crack!*—a noise directly overhead sounded louder than even the flames' roar: Clay looked up as a shower of flaming hay came raining down, but with something else amid it, something huge, heavy and solid—the loft crossbeam. The thought no sooner flashed in his brain than the great beam slammed into him, striking his shoulder and taking him down as easily as a grizzly bats a salmon from a falls. Clay felt the boy slip from his grasp, and now he lay on his face, his mouth pressed to the dirt. For a moment it felt welcome, cool, but then the pain caught up and the beam, the killing beam, unbelievably heavy across his bare right arm, was crushing it into the hard-packed ground and he couldn't pull free, pinned from shoulder to elbow.

David Shifren

CLAY'S JUSTICE

LEISURE BOOKS NEW YORK CITY

To E.D.K., for her endless encouragement and support.

A LEISURE BOOK®

November 2000

Published by

Dorchester Publishing Co., Inc.
276 Fifth Avenue
New York, NY 10001

ISBN 0-8439-4799-3

Printed in the United States of America.

CLAY'S JUSTICE

Chapter One

The animal's frightened bawls carried a good quarter mile—across the scrubby Montana range, up and down the dry-grassed hills, and through the scraggly chaparral to reach Clay on the trail. He reined in and listened, reckoning distance and direction: ahead, off-trail to the right, in that dip below the ridge.

Leaning into a bitter wind that whipped his pants legs and knifed down his coat collar, Clay scowled as he sat his mount. Someone's lost cow or calf was no business of his, and to reach Sharpton by nightfall he hadn't time to be chasing lost stock. Having slept in neither bed nor bunk in a week, he had his own concerns.

He twisted in his saddle and squinted back across the hills. No cattle, no riders. . . . Just graze-grass and rock-scrub as bleak and sorry-looking as to be expected after a winter this harsh. The late afternoon sun sat low on the horizon, a pale ball pinned in a gray sky that had done nothing to warm the day. Clay felt sorry he hadn't stopped over in Brayerville. He'd reached the town midday, but hadn't felt like passing the night in another broken-down one-horser, so like a hundred others he'd been through these past years. Now Sharpton was turning out to be farther away than he thought, which meant another night on the trail. Feeling hungry and stiff of muscle—a chill had crept into his bones so deep he felt it might never leave—Clay decided that tail-end-of-winter days weren't meant for riding windswept plains, let alone chasing down other people's stray animals.

Still, when the calf bawled again—a drawn-out peal not of immediate pain or danger, but of general distress—Clay shook his head and sighed. Drawing his reins sideways, he turned the Appaloosa's broad head toward the dip. *What the heck,* he thought. At least moving would warm his blood again.

He flicked leather.

He found the calf soon enough, just a few hundred yards down the slope, out of sight of the trail. Caught half across a barbed-wire fence, the three-month-old stood bleating plaintively, as a she-cow, no doubt its mother, stood beside it licking and nuzzling it. Clay rode up and mother and calf huddled closer, blinking at him blankly. He swung to the ground and looped his reins over the wire.

"Okay now, dogie, easy does it," Clay said. "Which goes for you, too, mama. . . ."

How the calf had managed to trap itself was plain.

Standing half across the middle strand, the silver wire snug against its loins, the animal obviously had decided to sample pasture on the far side, then gotten stuck midway. Clay patted the she-cow's flank, and, resting a gloved hand upon the younger animal, bent to one knee.

Where the dogie's belly rested between barbs on the twisted wire a tender-looking patch had rubbed raw. Clay slipped his arms beneath the calf, crooking its throat and rump with his elbows, and lifted. The animal bleated frighteningly, but Clay hugged it to keep it from struggling. Setting it down a moment later, he found its wound not deep, but needful of cleaning.

Pulling off his gloves, he unbuttoned his coat and unknotted his neck bandanna as he moved to his horse. He lifted the canteen from its leather cord looped over the horn, bit out its cork, and wet down the blue-checked cloth.

''Hold easy, now, fella,'' he said, returning to the animal and squeezing out the sopping bandanna. ''No, you *don't* know me, an' I don't know you. But let's get this done an' we can be on our separate ways again. . . .'' Clay knew easy patter would keep the calf calm, making the job quicker.

Where the animal's matted underbelly hair, stiff and wiry on even a calf this young, had been partly scraped away, Clay cleaned the tender area carefully.

''Should do it,'' he said some moments later, and straightened up.

Crack! The rifle shot sounded behind Clay and a geyser of dirt sprouted a yard from his boot toe.

Clay flung away the canteen and dove. Not that there was much to dive for—a shallow depression in the scrub grass was all, but it beat standing in place like a six-foot bull's-eye. Tasting grass in his mouth, he flashed on what he knew: the shot had come from a Winchester fired behind and slightly above him at about 150 yards. How he had registered this, he couldn't have said, nor, for that matter, did he remember reaching for his Colt, though it now lay in his hand, near enough his face for him to smell gun oil.

Carefully he raised his head.

Perhaps 160 yards off, the man with the rifle sat ahorse, facing him. His hat pulled low and the collar of his gray longcoat turned up, he held the Winchester across his legs. He sat just beyond accurate pistol range, as doubtless he had carefully gauged. Clay saw no other men—just the one shooter, then? Clay turned toward his Henry in its scabbard on the Appaloosa. Just a half-dozen yards away, yet those twenty feet might as well be a mile. The wind gusted, and Clay watched the grass riffle. A small tree's bare branches trembled. The mounted man's horse bowed its head and began a tight turn to position its rear to the chilling gust, but the rider steadied the animal expertly and, his hands still holding the rifle, he continued to face Clay.

"What you up to with my stock?" The man's voice was thin in the wind, yet it conveyed his anger.

Clay raised his head enough for his own voice to carry. "The calf was caught in the wire—I *freed* 'im!" He had had about enough. A man who fired on strangers showed poor manners as far as he was concerned. "You can put 'im back in now, if you want—I'm ready to ride. . . ."

The mounted man kept the rifle ready. "Not so fast! Lardon men got no business on my property!" This time the voice told Clay something more about the rifleman: He was an older man.

"Never heard a Lardon!" Clay called. "I'm just passin' through!"

The other man paused now, seeming a bit less sure. "You don't work for Brack Lardon?"

Trigger-happy fool, Clay thought. *Couldn't you asked me that five minutes ago?* "Listen, put up your rifle and I'll ride. I got no business with you."

The horseman seemed to consider. "No . . . no, you stand right where you are! I want a look at you."

Stand, thought Clay. *Not likely!*

"Tell you what, friend," he called. "In about ten minutes the sun's gonna be low enough for me to walk to that Appaloosa. I got a Henry in the boot that'll even things up, or you can rush me now, see how I handle a Colt. Choose one or the other, or ride in yourself or just ride out—but choose somethin'!"

The other man seemed to deliberate. But not for long. With the sky darkening by the minute, he couldn't dispute Clay's ultimatum. Clay saw the rider's heels rise slightly and drop against the gray's ribs, and slowly the animal started forward, its rider holding the Winchester at a ready angle. At fifty yards Clay cautiously rose, the pistol at his side aimed at the ground, but with its hammer thumbed back. Clay watched the mounted man come ahead.

The turned-up coat collar all but hid the rider's face, but the way he leaned slightly forward reinforced Clay's sense of him as not young. Clay noted his spindly legs astride the horse, a threadbare coat, and badly scuffed boots. At ten yards the man reined in, studying Clay in turn.

He marked a man some six feet tall, wide of shoulder and sturdily built, with a face long, creased, and unshaved. Where dark hair showed beneath his worn, gray Stetson, it looked shaggy and thick. Clay's hands, the horseman noted, were large and heavy-knuckled, a working man's shaped by toil. His blue-gray eyes held steady. In all, he looked like someone who had seen rough times, had risen to meet them, and would likely see more ahead, meeting them, too, without pause or complaint. He might have been thirty-three.

''Well,'' the rider admitted, ''I'll allow you don't look like any Lardon's men I know.''

Clay shook his head and frowned. ''You might'a asked before firing.'' His eyes on the mounted man, he shook his head and, trusting his instinct, reholstered his gun.

The other, too, put his weapon away, sliding the Winchester into its boot. Looking toward the calf now, the rider swung from his horse—somewhat stiffly, Clay noticed. Holding the reins in a gnarled, spotted hand, he walked to the calf. ''Do hisself much damage?''

Clay shook his head. ''Not much.''

Bending, the older man examined the animal.

"Stuck yourself on the wire, did you?" he asked, squinting at the raw spot.

"Half in, half out," said Clay.

"Fool dogie. That business about grass always lookin' greener? Musta been a cattleman said it first." After a moment, satisfied with the calf, he straightened to face Clay. Turning down his collar, the older man showed a face deep of line and white-whiskered, with rheumy eyes that shone pale blue when he pushed back his hat. "Guess I owe you an apology, mister! It's just—well, we've had some bad business 'round here lately, an' it leaves a man edgy. Sorry about the shootin'—not that I aimed to hit you. I was firin' low deliberate." Switching the reins to his left hand, he extended Clay his right. "Name's Cooke—Floyd Cooke."

Clay brought his hand from where it had been resting on his gun butt. "Will Clay," he said. They clasped hands.

Cooke nodded toward the calf and cow. "I keep thirty head or so, though it'll be a sight less after this winter. Been a bad one!"

"This your wire?" asked Clay.

The older man scowled. "I put 'er up last fall to keep out Brack Lardon's herd. His side runs way down to that birch grove you see." Cooke shook his head. "The man owns more land than anyone around, but keeps edgin' his animals to graze on other folks' property!" He scowled, and with wet blue eyes flashing, turned and spat deliberately across the wire. "Don't seem fair, but it's what I tell m' grandson all the time: 'Life *ain't* fair.' Can serve a man some hard pills to swallow, can't it?''

Clay squinted as if with his own thoughts. ''It surely can.''

The old man moved to his saddle, lifted a coiled rope from the horn, drew out the loop, and dropped it over the cow's head.

''Calf'll follow where she goes,'' Clay observed.

Cooke looked at him approvingly. ''You done some cattle work.''

Clay drew his gloves from his pocket and pulled them on. ''Along with just about everything else. . . .''

''I'm surprised to find anybody out this way this time a day,'' Cooke said. ''I came searchin' for them,'' he nodded at his animals, ''but you—well, like you said, it'll be dark soon. You headed to Sharpton?''

Clay nodded. ''Passed through Brayerville this morning an' sorry now I didn't stay over. Fella I talked to said Sharpton was close. I'm headed north to drive some cattle, figured I'd make Sharpton by nightfall, stay the night, then push on in the morning.''

''Sharpton's still a good half-day's ride.''

Clay nodded and turned to his horse. ''I guess I'll make camp, then—on your spread, if that's all right.'' He took his animal's reins from the wire.

''Listen, Clay,'' Cooke said, ''I'm obliged to you for helpin' the calf.'' The old man's eyes flicked toward the sky, gone deep gray now. ''It's cold an' gettin' colder. Why not stay at my place? It's just beyond the ridge, an' though it ain't much, my barn'll be a site warmer than the open plain. You're welcome to it for the night. 'Sides,'' he said with a smile, ''my wife'll have supper on. We don't eat fancy but we eat good, and you could probably stand some hot chow.''

Clay smiled. ''Don't want to trouble you, Cooke.''

''No trouble to it. 'Sides, you helped me an' fair's fair.''

Clay nodded. ''Well, I'll take you up—and thanks.''

''Floyd. You call me Floyd,'' Cooke said, and, tying the rope to his saddle, he mounted up. Clay did too, and the men rode out.

Chapter Two

The old man hadn't been lying. He'd called his settlement modest, and, as he and Clay rode in, Clay noticed even in the fading light the small shack's rough-weathered roof, its barn in sore need of paint, and the tiny corral's badly split crossrails.

"Ain't much to look at," Cooke said, following Clay's gaze, "but we do our best with what we got."

Clay nodded somberly. "I can see that." And see it he could. For as wanting as the small settlement was, and as plain a testimony to sparse living, its shabbiness wasn't from the neglect of laziness, Clay realized, but only lack of money. The yard was neat, the cabin's windows clean, and its porch freshly swept. Flowers grew in a small garden. Cooke and family obviously stretched all they had to the limit, and where they couldn't spend money they spent effort and time instead. All this Clay saw in a glance, and when he said, "The work you've put in shows," his tone bespoke an understanding that made the older man glance sideways at him appreciatively.

"The trick is," Cooke said, "tryin' to hold onto it. I lost a dozen head this winter, and with that buzzard Lardon's dirty dealings—"

"Hey, Gran'pap—Gran'pap!"

The men looked ahead to the barn, where a boy stood at its open door. Clamping a hand to his hat, he ran toward the riders as they crossed the yard.

"I put down straw for 'im like you said," the boy blurted breathlessly, vapor puffs rising from his mouth. Wearing a hand-me-down coat, a floppy-brimmed hat and mended trousers, he looked, Clay supposed, about twelve years old. "But he still seems awful cold. Ain't there something else to do?"

"Danny, that colt'll be fine," said Cooke. His tone kindly, the old man continued, "It's a pity about his mother, she was a fine mare, but that barn's plenty warm enough." Cooke winked at Clay. "A boy's first horse ain't to be took lightly, I know, but there's still chores to be done." Cooke reached down and handed the boy the rope. "Now you take this here mama an' her young inside."

The boy took the rope but stood looking at Clay.

"An' say howdy to our supper guest," Cooke added, half turning. "Danny, this is Mr. Will Clay. Clay—m'grandson."

The boy ducked his head and touched his finger to his hat brim as if carefully tutored. "Pleased to meet you, sir."

Clay nodded easily. "Howdy-do, son. Got a new colt, have you?"

The boy's serious expression gave way to an excited grin. "Two days old! He's gray and I named him Tall Boy. That's how he stands—I mean, tall for his age. He's still small now, of course. But I can call him Tall later, too."

Clay smiled. "I'd be glad for a look at 'im."

In the barn, a dozen cows occupied front stalls with another ten or so in back. When Clay and Cooke had tended their mounts and Danny had seen to the cow and calf, the boy said excitedly, "I can show you my colt now, Mr. Clay."

But Cooke placed a hand on his grandson's shoulder. "Time for supper, Dan. Your gram and sis are waitin' an' the food's hot. Never keep a hot meal waitin'. Ain't that right, Mr. Clay?"

"Just 'Clay' is fine," said the visitor. "And yep, I agree."

Outside, the sky had darkened to a deep gray. Across the valley the mountains rose dark and uneven, jagged ridges jutting to form a distant horizon. A half-dozen stars, the night's first, shone brightly, pinpoints of clean, white light. Clay raised his eyes as he and the others crossed the yard.

"See that bunch straight up from the corral post," he said to Danny, "looks like a spray a white buckshot? Sioux call it *kon-a-tonni*—splashing water."

Cooke squinted skyward. "Does sorta look like it, don't it?" he agreed.

"You talk Sioux?" the boy asked, looking at Clay.

"Picked it up in my scoutin' days," Clay admitted. "Stays with a man."

After washing at the standing pump—the icy water bracing on their faces and tingling where it ran down their collars—and after they had dried their hands by shaking them in the chill air, the three moved across the cold, hard-packed earth toward the cabin. To Clay, the yellow, lantern-lit windows and smoke rising from the chimney made the promise of four walls and a roof welcome, but they also stirred certain other feelings and memories that left him momentarily subdued.

But then the men's boots sounded deep and hollow on the porch planks, and the three walked in through the cabin door, as they swept off their hats.

At the center of the room stood a heavy wooden table covered with plates, bowls, and lidded crockpots. Twin lanterns hung from the ceiling's crossbeams, and above a fire flickering in the stone hearth hung a large black cookpot on a blackened swinghook. The smell of beef, potatoes, and fresh cornbread filled the room, and amid the light, warmth and aroma of hot food, Clay suddenly felt surprisingly at home.

"Lena," said Cooke, shrugging from his coat as the boy did likewise, "I hope you made plenty. We got a supper guest—Mister Will Clay, or Clay, as he goes by . . ."

A small woman standing at a cutting board near the wall turned to them, her hair as white as Cooke's. Wiping her hands on her blue-checked apron, she regarded Clay curiously.

"Mister Clay, is it?" she said.

His hat in hand, Clay bowed his head slightly. "Just Clay's fine, ma'am," he said. "And it's nice to make your acquaintance. If those flowers outside are yours, you've got a fine touch."

Immediately won over by the tall, polite-spoken young stranger who obviously had an eye for the finer things, Lena smiled warmly. "You call me Lena," she said.

"Clay lent a hand with a calf stuck in the fence," Cooke said, hanging their coats on pegs. "By gosh, I wish I didn't need that wire. Dang that Lardon."

"Floyd," Lena said sharply, "now you mind that tongue before company."

Cooke moved to the fire and spread his hands toward the flames. "Where's Cal?"

"Here, Gramps," sang a voice from the other room.

At the doorway appeared a young woman holding table napkins.

Perhaps twenty years old, she had waist-length, copper-hued hair that shined as if freshly brushed, and large, green eyes that sparkled beneath long lashes. Her green plaid dress showed her arms and figure to advantage, and Clay caught himself staring despite himself. Cooke had mentioned Danny had a sister, but Clay had assumed she'd be nearer the boy's age.

"Callie," said Cooke, "meet Will Clay. Clay— our granddaughter Callie, who happens to make the best corn bread in the valley."

"Pleased to meet you, Mr. Clay," Callie said, her

warm smile showing even white teeth. "Any credit for the corn bread goes to Gram, though. It's her recipe."

"I hope you brought an appetite," Lena said to the guest.

Clay grinned. "I seldom travel without it."

The meal was a feast, everyone passing plates and bowls and pitchers and mugs back and forth in a production Clay thought couldn't have gone smoother. When finally they were done, their plates empty and the smell of food lingering, Danny turned to his grandfather. "Can I go out to the barn now, Gramps?"

Cooke smiled at Clay and shook his head. "Boys and colts, no one's about to keep 'em apart, so why try?" He turned to his grandson. "Just don't wake 'im if he's asleep. Newborns need their rest."

Danny raced to the coat pegs, yanked his jacket free and wrestled into it.

"And don't be forgettin' your chores, Danny," Lena added. "Floyd, I had to set the kerosene tin on the buckboard myself this morning. If you'd drove to town for supplies, you would never have knowed to buy fuel and we'd be sittin' here in the dark."

"Sorry, ma'am!" the boy shouted, even as he bolted out the door, slamming it behind him.

Cooke moved slowly to the mantle, taking up a pipe. "Like to join me?" he asked Clay. "I got a spare corncob 'round here someplace."

Clay shook his head. "No, thanks. I like to let a fine meal like that sit on its own awhile."

"Thank you, Mr. Clay," Lena said.

"Lena," Clay said, "now you gotta stop callin' me mister."

Lena smiled. "*Will,* then. But do tell, what brings you out this way?"

Clay sat back. "Like I told Floyd, I'm headed north to hire on with a cattle drive. They'll be leavin' next month."

"Is that the main work you do?" Callie asked. Clearing the table, she was stacking dishes for Lena, who stood at a large, galvanized metal tub, working up suds.

"Now, Callie," Lena said, her sleeves rolled to her elbows. "Don't be pryin' with all sorts a questions." Lena seemed to forget that the first question had been hers.

Clay smiled. "I appreciate the interest." He turned to Callie. "I've drove my share of cattle, but I've also ranched and rodeoed—done some deputyin', too."

"A deputy's what we could use around here," said Cooke, "and an honest sheriff. I think the one we got is in Lardon's pocket."

"That so?" Clay asked.

"It's like I said outside," Cooke began, gripping the pipe more tightly in his knobby fist where he sat at the table. "Lardon owns more'n anyone around yet won't rest happy 'til he's grabbed up the whole valley. And things were 'specially tough this winter."

"Hard hit, were you?" Clay asked.

"Every outfit I know lost stock—the Double-J, Zem Keen down the ridge, old Tad Johnson. . . ."

Cooke shook his head. "But Lardon just let a few hands go and it's business as usual." Cooke puffed hard on the pipe. "Worst part is, when spring comes he'll charge sky-high for water like last year when the stream run dry. Some a the smaller ranches have already sold out to 'im at terrible low prices."

"There's enough graze-land in this valley for everyone," said Callie, pausing in drying a bowl. "But Brack Lardon wants it all and has been pressuring people to sell out. He's a selfish, greedy, conniving—"

"Callie," said Lena. "Watch your language! Floyd, she learns it from you."

Cooke pounded the table with his fist. "An' she's right! A snake by any other name—"

"He bleeds people dry!" Callie blurted, the color rising in her face.

"He'd like *me* to sell," Cooke said, but it'll be a cold day in—"

"Floyd!" Lena said.

"A *cold* day," Cooke said, " 'fore I sell to Brack Lardon."

Callie beamed at her grandfather proudly. "Grandpa was one of the first in this valley," she said to Clay. "He helped settle it and the others still look to him."

"All right now, the two of you," said Lena. "Will's heard all he needs to about the Cookes for one night." She turned to the visitor. "You got to excuse 'em, Will, we don't get many visitors, which you can understand now."

"Well," Callie suggested, "then let's hear about Mr. Clay."

Clay shook his head. "Oh, well, now, I don't want to bore everyone."

"That never stopped Floyd," Lena sniffed.

"Watch it, woman," the old man growled, mock-threateningly.

"Seriously, though, Mr. Cl—Will," Callie said, catching herself.

Clay shrugged. "It's not much've a story. My folks died of cholera when I was small an' I grew up with my uncle and aunt. They had no kids of their own, so when they died in the Fort Beacon raid, and all they had owned was taken or burned, I lit out with the clothes on my back and a horse. I was sixteen and took work where I found it."

"Life can be hard when no one hands you nothin'," Cooke observed, puffing his pipe. "But like I said, unfairness is just in the nature of things, without rhyme nor reason."

"Oh, there's reason," said Lena. " 'For all things under heaven a purpose,' says the Good Book. We just may not understand the reason."

"Woman," said Cooke, "I'd like to know the reason for a thousand head a cattle dyin' across this range this winter. And for that matter, what about Helen and Frank?"

"Now, Floyd," Lena said, "don't get started."

Floyd turned to Clay. "Callie and Dan come to us twelve years ago, her seven or eight an' him no more than a swaddling baby after their ma and pa—our daughter, Helen, and her husband—died in a fire.

Now, the young'uns livin' with us has been a blessing, no question, but their ma and pa were good, decent folks—and not just 'cause they were kin. So if there's justice in the world, I'd like someone to tell me why they died."

"Oh, Floyd," Lena said.

"Got no answer, have you, woman?" Floyd said. He turned to Clay. "We fight on this all the time. Me, I say it'd be nice to think everyone gets their just deserts, but I just don't see it happenin'."

"But doesn't it come down to the law?" asked Callie. "When you need justice done, you go to the law?"

Cooke smiled at Clay. "That's our Callie: She's good so she thinks everyone is." Cooke rapped his pipe against the table. "The law don't always work, honey. Not man's law, which can get bought."

"What do you think, Will?" asked Callie.

"About life servin' people what they deserve?" Clay sighed deeply, then shook his head. "I'm afraid I agree with your granddad." He grew serious. "Sometimes things happen—tragedies—there seems no reason for. You do nothing to cause 'em, don't know what you might be bein' punished for, and there's not a thing you can do to change 'em. I guess the idea is just to learn to live with 'em. It's all you *can* do, or go crazy." Clay was staring into the fire.

For a moment everyone was quiet. Then Callie asked softly, "Did you ever have a wife, Clay?"

"*Callie,*" said Lena, "what did I say about pryin'?" But the old woman's tone carried little conviction; plainly she was as interested as her granddaughter in hearing their guest's reply.

Clay glanced toward the younger woman and smiled gently. "I was married once." His eyes turned to the quietly burning logs. "Her name was Rachel. She lived with her folks and we met at a barn dance. I finally got some money together, an' some land, an' after about a year of seein' each other we got married. Soon she was with child. Then one night, with the baby not due for months yet, she started havin' these pains." Clay sighed mightily. "By time the doctor got there the baby'd come, but Rachel . . . didn't make it. The baby died the next week. A little boy. I remember I kept askin' myself, Why? She was good a person as I ever knew, better than me, so why her? I couldn't stay there with everything remindin' me of our plans, so I sold for less than it was worth to get out fast." Clay squinted as a burning log slipped. "I been riding ever since. Stayin' here awhile, there awhile . . . It hasn't seemed to matter much where, one place always like another. It's been, oh, two years now." He shook his head. Then suddenly he looked up, and cleared his throat as if embarrassed, a man unaccustomed to talking who realized suddenly that he had said much. "Like I said, it's not much of a story."

"Clay," said Lena, "I told Callie not to pry but now I'm going to do it myself—I guess that's an old woman's right. Listen, movin' from place to place won't cure sadness that's inside you. 'No matter where you go, there you are,' haven't you heard that?

You got to let what's past *pass*—especially after a year, two years . . .''

Cooke drew the pipe from his mouth. ''Now, Lena, go easy on the man,'' he said gently.

''No, that's all right,'' said Clay. He looked up at the old woman. ''What you say holds a lot of truth. I'd always thought as long as I had my two legs to walk on and two hands, things could never get but so bad. But I guess this just proved I was wrong.''

''We seen our share a bad times, too,'' Lena said, shaking her head. ''But a body's just gotta carry on . . . And trust in the Lord.'' Suddenly she looked up. ''Goodness, is that boy still in the barn? He'd sleep there if we let 'im. Callie, run out and fetch him.''

But Clay rose to his feet first. ''Listen, I'm about ready to turn in. I'll just send 'im on in.''

''Now wait, Will,'' said Lena. ''You're not sleeping in that drafty barn when there's room in the house!''

''I don't mind,'' Clay said. ''A roof's more than I expected and I've got my sleeping roll.''

''Purge the thought from your mind!'' said Lena. She turned to her granddaughter. ''Callie, you'll sleep in our room. Floyd, you haul in her mattress. Danny can sleep on the bench-seat cushions on the floor in his room, and that leaves Clay Danny's bed.'' She turned to the houseguest. ''See? Plenty a room!''

Clay smiled. ''Well, I'll head out and get Danny, then.''

''And bring in any of your things you'll need,'' said Lena. ''There's plenty a room in the pantry.''

* * *

Clay pulled the door closed as he stepped out onto the porch. After the warmth of the cabin the chill night air felt refreshing. Standing on the porch, he fixed himself a smoke.

After these months on the trail, the company of others felt more welcome than he might have guessed or almost cared to admit. Sure, there'd been cowboys enough—wranglers and rodeo-riders, drifters and saddlebums—but it wasn't the same as womenfolk and a youngster. Tonight's dinner, and the talk after, reminded him of things he'd wanted in his own life once, but had long since stopped thinking about, let alone desiring. Or so he told himself. Was a family something you could miss before you'd even had one?

In any case, one thing about tonight had certainly surprised him: How he'd run on at the mouth! Saying more than he'd have guessed he even had to say. The family just seemed so easy to talk to.

For a moment his thoughts turned to Rachel. Having married later in life than some men, he had yet been widowed in it so early. No, it didn't seem fair.

Flicking the cigarette to the dirt, Clay stepped off the porch and crushed the glowing orange tip with his boot. Taking long strides, he headed toward the barn.

Chapter Three

The tall, well-oiled barn door swung open easily and Clay felt the warm air from the animals and smelled the hay. He drew the door closed behind him, seeing where soft yellow light showed from a rear stall past the shadows of animals standing asleep. Making his way back, Clay found the youngster sitting in a rear stall, a newborn colt standing awkwardly beside him.

''This is smart,'' Clay said. ''Keeping him back from the draft of the door.''

''That's what gramps said,'' replied Danny, nodding.

On the ground beside the boy stood a lantern. Clay bent and grasped its handle.

''You want to hang this from a peg, though,'' he said, while doing so. ''This hay's dry.''

The boy nodded. "Yessir—sorry!" The small, dark colt stood on gangly legs, its enormous eyes looking at Clay.

"He's handsome," Clay admitted. "You know a colt's born with full-grown eyes? That's why they look so big—that's a horse's eyes in a colt's face."

"I just hope he's healthy," the boy said. "There was another born for me last year, but she died almost right away. That's why I been waitin' for him."

Clay moved to the colt, which raised its head with nostrils delicately flaring as it sniffed. Clay looked closely at the animal's eyes, then placed his hand on its back and bent to rest his ear against the colt's warm chest. After a moment Clay straightened up. "Got a good, strong heart . . . seems sturdy. . . . He should grow to be a fine animal." Clay looked down at the boy and smiled. "C'mon son, it's late. Let's head in."

Clay lifted the lantern from the hook and, carrying it, sent shadows around the barn. As they went out, he stopped to check the Appaloosa. He patted the animal then moved to his saddle and gear thrown astraddle a rail and took his sleeping roll and saddlebags.

"What if he gets hungry?" asked the boy, as they made their way to the door.

"He'll be fine 'til mornin'."

They went out and the wind grabbed at them.

"But you think he'll be warm enough?" Danny asked.

"With that stall full of hay? Don't worry. Here, why don't you carry the lantern?"

Clay walked with his gear over one shoulder and his free hand resting on the youngster's shoulder.

Clouds scuttled across the moon throwing the grassland into shadow as the two riders made their way across the hills.

"Rax, get down off that ridge!"

The man named Rax—twenty-five years old, solidly built, with his hat pulled low over long, unbrushed blond hair—guided his horse down off the hillcrest, his silhouette merging with the other man's in the gloom.

"Who you afraid's gonna see us, Morgan? You think anyone else is out in this dang cold?"

Dirk Morgan spoke over his shoulder. "I'm takin' no chances, which means you ain't, neither. You forget what we're out here for?"

"I ain't forgot nothin'," said Rax, as he turned and spat into the darkness.

The men continued on, tree leaves brushing their coats and hats as their horses plodded along the narrow deer trails. Dirk Morgan, in the lead—in his mid-thirties, with several days' beard growth, a bushy mustache and dark, unsmiling eyes—said nothing more.

As they rode, the large, rectangular metal can tied by its handle to the younger man's pommel kept bumping his leg. Coupled with the bitter cold, it soured Rax's mood even more than usual.

"I just wanna know when we're gonna get there," he muttered. "We been ridin' for hours. I thought they live close."

''Wipe your nose and stop your bellyachin',''
Morgan snapped disgustedly. ''What're you, some snot-nosed kid?''

Rax glared at the other man's back. ''You sure we ain't lost?''

Morgan didn't bother to turn. He just muttered something and spat.

During the rest of the ride the men said no more, the sole sound of their travel now the plodding of the horses' hooves, the rhythmical creak of saddle leather and a soft sound of liquid sloshing in the can. It wasn't until a half-hour later, at the edge of the wood, that Morgan finally reined in.

''There she is,'' he said. ''Down in the clearing . . .''

To Rax it looked the same as everyplace else, trees overhead shutting out the moon, the trail ahead but a pale, curving line. But then he saw them—a pair of distant, moonlit buildings: one a cabin, the other, with the dark lines of a corral fence behind it, plainly a barn.

From their cover in the wood, the two men sat gazing down at the sleeping Cooke settlement.

Danny lay awake, eyes wide, staring at the ceiling. Lying on cushions on the floor, he just couldn't fall asleep—didn't feel sleepy at all. The night was cold, but that wasn't it—under double blankets pulled to his eyes he felt warm enough. No, he was thinking of Tall Boy. The colt must be freezing. Drawing the edge of the blanket down to his chin, Danny felt the chilly air across his face. If it were this cold in the house, how much colder must the barn be? Gran'pop had said the colt would be fine, but remembering how Tall Boy had shivered before Danny'd thrown down the hay, and imagining how drafty the dark barn must get, Danny wasn't sure. He closed his eyes and listened for sounds from the barn, and he imagined he could hear something—through the heavy barn door, across the wide yard, and through the closed bedroom window—a faint, distant nickering: Tall Boy!

Danny turned toward Clay. Across the room in the boy's bed, beneath a heavy wool blanket, the dark, sleeping form looked huge. Gram had offered him extra blankets, but Clay had said his own bedroll would do, and he'd brought it in from the pantry where he'd stored the rest of his gear. As Clay breathed in long, regular breaths, Danny turned again toward the ceiling.

Well, he had to do something for Tall Boy. If only its mother had survived! Without her, the tiny colt was all alone. But what could Danny do? Then it came to him: *Blankets.* He would bring the colt some.

Looking again across the room at Clay, the boy drew his covers aside and slipped out from them. Draping one blanket across his shoulders and clutching the other to his chest, he moved to the bureau—all the while watching Clay, and stepping carefully to avoid the floorboards that creaked. Danny found the small lantern that sat there easily enough, but discovered no matches. He remembered seeing the box on the mantel in the other room. With the blankets filling his arms, the lantern seemed more trouble than it was worth, so he carefully set it back down.

Surely the moonlight would light his way. He began toward the door then stopped, remembering the badly squeaking bottom hinge. Gran'pop had been after him to oil it, but he hadn't gotten around to it. He wished now that he had. Danny looked again toward Clay, deliberated a moment, then changed course for the window.

Grasping the sash handle, he drew the window slowly toward him. But when it creaked, a voice sounded immediately from the darkness.

"What you up to, son?"

Danny spun and dimly saw Clay lying on one elbow.

"I think I hear Tall Boy!" the youngster said in an urgent, nervous whisper.

There was a pause. "The colt? You *hear* him?"

"I think so. I think he's cold!"

"A horse can stand it cooler than a person," said Clay patiently. "Horses, cattle, dogs—they got their winter coats."

The boy was quiet. "But he's so little. . . . I thought I could bring him some extra blankets . . ."

In the darkness Clay smiled. That the boy felt responsible for a creature in his care was good. It would serve him later. "Well," Clay said, "why don't you go ahead . . ."

"Really?" the boy blurted. Quickly he turned and opened the window wide.

"Just don't be long," Clay said. "Is that a deal?"

"I promise!" the boy said, and gathered the blankets in his arms.

"You don't want to use the door?"

"Well . . . Callie sleeps awful light."

Clay chuckled. "Fair enough."

Reaching out, the boy dropped the blankets to the ground and carefully slipped out after them.

The ground was hard and cold beneath Danny's bare feet. Pulling the window closed, the boy gathered up the blankets, then stood waiting a moment for his eyes to adjust to the moonlight. When he could see the barn clearly, he arranged the blankets across his back again and started forward.

He made his way across the yard easily enough, his shadow skimming the ground just ahead of him. With the blankets across his back and clutched to his chest his shadow looked huge, like some grizzly out hunting dinner, and he quickened his pace. Once, he stepped on a stone that jabbed sharply into the middle of his heel; he nearly cried out, but, bending his head, he pressed his face into the blanket and hissed sharply between clenched teeth. The thick, coarse material muffled not only the sound, but, Danny thought, also the pain.

At the barn door he looked back to see the house still dark. He drew the door open and the next moment stood inside, pulling it closed.

The warmth was surprising. It *was* warmer than he'd have guessed, far warmer than outside. The familiar smells of horse sweat, hay, and manure felt somehow reassuring and once again the boy stood blinking to adjust to the change in light. In the gloom he heard the animals stir uneasily, sensing his presence.

''Sh-h-h, now,'' he said, adopting the even tone his grandfather used. ''Settle down, now. . . . E-e-asy . . .''

The barn was truly pitch-black. Danny felt sorry now he didn't have the lantern after all. Clutching the blanket at his chest, he moved slowly forward, lightly running his fingers along the stall dividers, barely skimming the wood for fear of splinters. He proceeded toward the back of the barn sensing the huge animals on either side, their shapes large and dark; they breathed deeply, occasionally sleepily stamping a heavy hoof or shifting position where they leaned against the worn old boards between stalls, making the thin wood creak. Overhead, Danny could make out shocks of pale gray hay overhanging the loft.

At last he reached the rear stall. Slipping a hand between the slats, he held it steady, and heard a gentle shuffling sound of movement. Then moist air warmed his fingers. He lifted his hand gently and felt the colt's soft nose.

''Hi, Tall Boy,'' Danny whispered. ''Don't worry—it's me. Shh!'' Danny crept closer. If he didn't look directly ahead, but slightly turned his head, at the corner of his eye he could make out the colt's small dark form.

''Look what I brought!'' said the boy. Feeling for the latch, he went in, then secured the gate again. He patted Tall Boy's soft head. ''This'll keep you warm for sure.'' He moved to the rear of the stall, dropping to his knees to arrange the blankets over the hay. The colt came to him and he settled the animal down, then sat cross-legged in the hay beside it and stroked its neck.

After a while Danny shivered, and moved closer to the colt. He drew the edge of the blanket over his legs and settled in beside the sleeping animal. The hay against the boy's neck felt briefly scratchy, but then became warm and even comfortable. Outside, the wind whistled sharply, but here, under the high-pitched roof, only the regular breathing of the animals sounded. Soon the boy's breath blended smoothly with the other creatures'.

Chapter Four

"Take care to tie 'im extra good," Morgan said.

The two men were securing their horses to an aspen sapling two hundred yards from the Cooke shack. Following his partner's advice, Rax wound his animal's reins an extra turn around the limb.

"We do what we came for," Morgan continued, "we'll be headed out fast. Your animal's wandered off somewheres, you sure ain't doublin' up with me." Morgan pulled his collar up further, then found the side flap where his coat opened over his holster; he slid the Colt up and down in its leather several times.

"You expectin' anything I don't know about?" Rax asked.

"Habit," said Morgan. "Without habits like this

you'll be dead 'fore long. . . . Now grab the can an' let's go."

In the silver light of a moon half hidden by clouds, the two made their way along the edge of the wood keeping to cover. Beyond the trees, the two buildings rose silhouetted against the pale ground. The riders proceeded toward the rear of the barn, keeping the larger building between themselves and the shack.

"Anybody in the house can't sleep," Morgan explained, "we don't want 'em seein' us out a window."

When finally they reached the spot where they would leave the wood, Morgan warned, "Now keep that can close to your leg. Don't let the moon shine on 'er—"

"*That's* what I could use some of," said the younger man, "*Moonshine!*"

Morgan scowled. "An' take *them* things off!"

Rax stopped. "Huh?"

"Them spurs, weasel brain. Take 'em off."

Rax glanced toward the house, some sixty yards off. "They can't hear nothin'. You worry too much."

"It's worryin' keeps me alive. Now take 'em off!"

Rax's eyes narrowed. Morgan had been ordering him around since the beginning of this, and Rax had had just about enough. "Get off my back, Morgan. Who made you boss?"

Morgan eyed the glaring man closely. The young idiot would get them both killed if Morgan let him. But now wasn't the time to press the issue. "All right," the older man said. "Just get a move on . . ."

Stepping carefully, they crossed the yard. As they approached the looming building, first the horizontal lines of the corral fence, then the squat black rectangle of a water trough, and finally the dully gleaming surface of a freestanding pump beside the house all became distinct.

At the back of the barn they peered around its corner toward the shack. Sitting quiet and dark, it looked all but deserted. Morgan was pleased when the large, wide barn door swung open noiselessly; cracking it just enough for the two men to squeeze through, he pulled it shut behind them. In the darkness they stood listening a moment. Then a sharp, sparking pop sounded, and a rasping hiss, and the flaring match Morgan's fingers held illumined their surroundings. When it subsided a moment later, it cast a feeble glow that showed the dark, glittering eyes and perked ears of several animals and the wide, dark rumps of others.

"That's a decent-looking Appaloosa," said Rax, pointing to a nearby stall. "Be a waste to leave 'im—how 'bout I take 'im?"

"An' get spotted with 'im next week," said the other man flatly. "Listen, Rax, save yourself the trouble a thinkin' an' just do your job." Morgan drew a second match from his shirt pocket and lit it on the dying first.

Rax unscrewed the can's cap and, upending the tin, began splashing its contents onto the planked walls; immediately a smell of kerosene filled the air. Moving to the nearest stalls, Rax doused the dry wood, the cows shying back from the smell. Up and back Rax moved, splashing the volatile liquid.

"In back, too," directed Morgan, nodding toward the gloomy rear of the building. But Rax raised the can high.

"Empty," he said. "She'll spread fast, though, don't worry." And with that he flung the empty can aside where it struck the ground with a hollow thunk.

Danny started awake. A noise had woke him, although he couldn't say what. He realized he lay still in the barn, but when a voice sounded, and it wasn't Gramps, he felt confused. Another voice sounded. Both were harsh. Danny kept still. Then he smelled . . . kerosene, was it? Blinking, he realized that a glow of light shone at the front of the barn. Beside him the colt nickered softly. Danny clamped a hand to its nostrils.

"Shh!" he whispered, his mouth at the creature's ear. Carefully rising, keeping his head low, the boy peered above the wooden stall divider.

Ten yards from where he crouched, two strangers stood. Danny's heart jumped. As he stared wide-eyed, one of the men took a step toward the door and flicked the match he was holding into a shining puddle. A loud *whoosh!* sounded as a wave of flame fanned out low across the ground, illuminating the barn and sending a black cloud curling toward the loft. Danny gasped. He had to tell gran'pop, but he also realized he was cornered, his escape route blocked. Should he wait until the men left? But by then it might be too late.

Measuring the distance to the door, Danny leaped up and bolted.

"Gramps!" he shouted. *"Gramps!"*

The men's heads snapped sharply toward him, their orange-lit faces showing surprise. Danny didn't stop to look. He was racing past the nearer, younger-looking man.

"Fire!" Danny yelled again, but then the man snaked out a hand and grabbed the boy's arm. Danny wrenched free. *"Gramps!"*

The man cursed and grabbed Danny again, but the boy twisted around, swinging wildly with both fists. One caught the man on the side of the face—Danny felt the hardness of bone—and the man swore again, and stumbled, and Danny tripped. Both went down, and Danny's head struck the edge of one of the gates. The boy lay still.

"Dang!" blurted Rax, back on his feet and panting. "Where'd *he* come from?!"

Morgan was at the door. The smoke was getting thick and the animals were moving frightenedly, their eyes big.

"Who knows. C'mon, let's get outta here!"

"You think anybody heard?"

"I ain't waitin' to find out!"

"What about him? We gonna leave 'im?"

"He *saw* us . . . saw us both! C'mon, let's go!"

With that Morgan disappeared out the door. Rax immediately followed, shoving the door closed behind him.

Chapter Five

Clay snapped open his eyes thinking: *wolf? Cougar?* What had begun as the sound of restless cattle lowing, changed, then, to a fretful bleating, finally to become the full-fledged bawls of terror they were now, had been filtering through his sleeping brain for some moments. Now fully awake, he realized that no, no prowling cougar or wolf was spooking the herd, for there was no herd: Clay was on no cattle drive, but abed in the Cooke cabin, with the frightened-sounding cattle out in the barn. Looking across the room, Clay discerned the dim outline of the boy's makeshift bed. Empty. Danny had gone to check on the colt, but how long ago? And even as these questions prodded at Clay, the first, more troubling one—of why the cattle were crying so—prompted him to flip his blanket aside and rise from bed. The night air chilled his bare skin and the rough floorboards cooled his feet as he tugged on trousers and moved to the window.

With the moon up, Clay could see easily across the yard. All looked peaceful enough. But then—was that a glimmer of light inside the barn? And there—another? He pulled open the window, and immediately caught a scent that made his blood rush: *Burning hay.* And through the open air he now also heard thumping noises—muffled sounds of heavy hooves kicking at stalls and the sharp crack of boards splintering.

"Oh, *no*," Clay whispered hoarsely, and then he was moving, pivoting from the window, yanking open the bedroom door.

"Cooke!" he shouted. "*Cooke!* Your barn's afire!" In the tiny hall he pounded on the other door. "Cooke!"

"What . . . hey . . . ?" The old man's voice was sleep-thick, but the women's voices sounded then, too, clipped and imperative.

"Floyd! Wake up!"

"Gramps! It's a *fire*!"

Clay called sharply, "Is Danny in there with you?!"

"No!" shot back Callie.

And again Clay was moving, pivoting from the door, striding across the room to yank open the front door, cross the porch and leap to the dirt with bare feet to cut sharply across the yard.

In the moonlight, columns of thick gray smoke rose from the barn roof like steam after a rain. Clay cursed, knowing it meant the loft had caught; the roof would soon follow. Orange-yellow light flickered the length of the building at every crack.

"Danny!" Clay shouted. "Dan!"

Through the barn door the cattle's cries sounded high-pitched and panicked, filling Clay's ears even as Lena's anguished screams sounded from behind: *"Danny!"*

Seizing the heavy wooden latch and jerking it upward, Clay yanked hard, swinging the wide door open quaveringly. It was like opening the gate to Hades. Out billowed black smoke so thick the very cloud itself seemed alive with the animals' shrieks.

"Danny!" Clay shouted. Then something came rushing at Clay, a huge form moving fast. Clay dodged aside as from the eye-broiling conflagration burst a large bull, shooting past, a dozen cows behind it stampeding for air, rushing past with heads high, nostrils wide, eyes rolling, and tongues stretched out as they bawled in terror.

Seeing a break in their numbers, Clay threw himself amid them, his body slim among their huge, jostling ones, his bare white feet darting among the crushing hooves. The next moment he was inside.

And here it was a hundredfold worse, for there was no air, only thick, choking smoke, closing Clay's eyes to slits. He gasped as the acrid air seared his nostrils and lungs. Half crouching, his eyes already past tearing, he fought to see through the hot air aswirl with cinders. *"Danny!"* Clay shouted again into the roaring inferno.

Around him huge shadowy figures reared and bellowed, straining against loudly cracking, smoking wood. Clay crouched to stay beneath the thickest smoke and suddenly found a huge cow blocking his way, the animal frozen in terror.

"Gid-out!" Clay shouted through cracked lips, as with an open hand he struck the animal hard across its flanks. The beast flinched but didn't move, and Clay brought his hand down again harder yet, and this time the animal wheeled, its forehooves off the ground, and bolted for the black rectangle of night beyond the door. Other cattle, less lucky, thrashed and leaped in their stalls, falling broadside across the wooden stall dividers, smashing wood and ribs, their cries and bellows combining with the roar of the flames. Clay's horse bolted past him toward the door.

Suddenly Clay saw a form lying in the dirt. He rushed to it, but found it to be a calf. As Clay rose, a bull burst from an adjacent stall, broadsiding him hard with its shoulder. Clay went sprawling. In the inferno's light, among the lurching shadows, he saw another form stretched on the ground—and this time it *was* the boy, lying on his face. Clay flipped him over, scooped him in his arms, and straightened. His lungs were on fire now and his stinging eyes all but sealed shut. *The door's back that way,* he thought. *Straight back . . .*" If he were wrong, he knew there would be no second guess—not with his temples throbbing and his face feeling like an overripe tomato about to burst in the sun. Clay spun and took a first step, when *crack!*—a noise directly overhead sounded louder than even the flames' roar: Clay looked up as a shower of flaming hay came raining down, but with something else amid it, something huge, heavy and solid—the loft crossbeam. The thought no sooner flashed in his brain than the great beam slammed into him, striking his shoulder and taking him down as easily as a grizzly bats a salmon from a falls. Clay felt the boy slip from his grasp, and now he lay on his face, his mouth pressed to the dirt. For a moment it felt welcome, *cool,* but then the pain caught up and the beam, the killing beam, unbelievably heavy across his bare right arm, was crushing it into the hard-packed ground and he couldn't pull free, pinned from shoulder to elbow. With all his strength he strained, pushing against the ground with his other hand, with his legs, then scrabbled at the glowing wood with his left hand. But it was no good, and his lungs felt they'd burst and his head pounded. And he thought, *To die twenty feet from safety? And for the boy to die, too? No!* But the beam wouldn't budge.

Then something wet slapped across his neck. He managed to turn his head, and something wet fell there, too, over his face so that he sputtered and coughed.

"Hold on!" shouted a voice in his ear. And now he saw Cooke and Callie, with steaming towels draped over their heads and held to their faces, crouched beside him.

"He's pinned, Gramps!" Callie shouted.

"Help me with the beam, Cal! Together—*now!*" And Clay felt the terrible pressure on his arm shift and lessen, but only for an instant before it returned worse than ever. He grunted. Then a second time it shifted and returned. But the third time the weight lessened and stayed gone and he heard the beam thump on the ground beside his head. Cooke shouted, "Okay! Cal, you drag Danny out!"

Then hands grabbed Clay firmly beneath his arms, and he saw his heels run grooves in the dirt as Cooke dragged him backward.

And then he was outside, and the coolness made his teeth chatter.

"Lena! More towels!" shouted Cooke.

And lying on his back squinting up at the pinpricks of stars, Clay thought how cool the black sky looked. *Kon-a-tonni,* he thought.

And then the stars blinked out.

Chapter Six

He was seated at his desk when the knock sounded.

"Yeah!" Brack Lardon growled. He leaned back in his overstuffed, green leather chair, scowling around the cigar clenched in his teeth, the stogie's smoke rising in short, sharp puffs toward the cross-beamed ceiling. "Come in!" he shouted, in a voice used to giving orders.

The heavy study door swung inward.

The rough-looking man standing there, tall, powerfully built perhaps thirty wore a soiled yellow-checked shirt and stained chaps. His dark eyes sat deep-set in his unshaved face and a wedge of brown hair sliced diagonally across his forehead. Although his thick neck and big hands—with knobby knuckles that had obviously been broken a number of times—

suggested he was a fighter, he wore a gunbelt as well. ''They just rode in.''

''Good. Send 'em here,'' said the seated man. As the other turned, Lardon added, ''But don't go far, Boose. I don't put it past those two to try something.''

The big man went out.

Brack Lardon, fifty-two years old, short but built thick, with heavy shoulders and shaggy gray brows, opened a desk drawer and removed two small leather pouches knotted with rawhide drawstrings. The way he hefted them showed them to be of weight. One he set on the desk, the other he weighed in his palm even as boots sounded on the hardwood floor outside the door. The next moment, in stepped Dirk Morgan and Fred Rax. Not removing their hats, they walked to the center of the room.

''It's done,'' said Morgan.

''Sure is!'' agreed Rax.

Lardon nodded, still weighing the pouch. ''Any trouble?''

Rax glanced sidelong at Morgan, but Morgan kept his eyes on the rancher. ''We left the barn burnin',''' he said. ''We looked back from up the ridge and the roof was near gone. That's our end.''

Lardon eyed him, then nodded. ''Fair enough.''

''She was burnin', all right,'' said Rax suddenly, grinning darkly. ''But I think we oughtta get a few extra dollars for our extra trouble. . . .''

''Rax!'' snapped Morgan, shooting him a look.

Lardon squinted from one man to the other. ''What's this?''

The younger man grinned recklessly and turned to his partner. "Listen, Morgan, he'll find out tomorrow anyway, and the way I see it, he owes us somethin' for our extra risk!"

The ranch owner was suddenly standing. "Morgan! What's he talking about?"

Morgan shrugged. "There was a kid in the barn. He started hollerin' an' would have woke everybody. . . ."

"Won't shout no more, though, will he, Morgan?" asked the younger man slyly.

Lardon's brow darkened as he turned to Morgan. "What're you sayin'? You *killed* 'im?"

Morgan growled. "He fell an' hit his head. We left 'im so's we wouldn't get caught settin' *your* fire!"

"An' you figured you just wouldn't say anything?" asked the rancher.

"Nobody saw us," said Morgan. "That's what counts."

"What *counts,*" said Lardon angrily, "is that you do what I tell you! Whose land is this? Whose ranch? Some kid gets killed, people're gonna wanna know how. We're talkin' murder! An' what when they come nosin' around my door?"

"Nobody's nosin' nowhere," snarled Morgan.

"Yeah, so like I said," interrupted Rax, sensing things weren't going as he'd hoped, "seems to me we got some extra money comin'. . . ."

Lardon shot the younger man a look. "Extra, huh? For givin' me something extra to worry about, that how you figure?" The rancher's face went dark.

"Who knows what you two'll bollix up next! Listen, I want you out—the both a you!"

He suddenly flung the pouch he had been holding to the floor; the bag split open and several gold coins spilled out, rolling across the wood ringingly.

"Say!" exclaimed Rax, quickly bending to collect them.

"All right, get out—now! The both a you!" Lardon ordered.

But Morgan remained standing there eyeing the rancher coolly.

"We got the other pouch still comin'," he said. "That was the deal."

"Deal's broke," Lardon shot back. "You broke it by not followin' orders."

Rax, having gathered the loose coins, slowly straightened. "Listen, Lardon," he began. "You got to do right by us—"

"Or *what*?" said the rancher. "You gonna tell the law? Turn me in?" He smiled darkly. "Who you think they'll string up first? You'll have a noose around your neck so fast you won't know who put it there!"

Morgan had been hanging slightly back. "This ain't the way for it to be, Lardon."

Lardon stepped boldly from behind the desk. He wore no gun, yet his manner suggested he held aces. "You don't get another nickel. You're useless to me now. Get outta my sight."

But the younger man stood firm. "I say we get what's ours," he said flatly. His eyes on the rancher, he took a half step to his left to face the man eye-to-eye. The pouch of coins he'd stuffed into his shirt left his hands free; now his right hovered loosely near his sidearm.

Lardon looked at Rax a long moment. Then he growled, "Boose?"

"Right here," came a voice from the doorway. Although low, even relaxed, its undertone of menace made its threat clear.

Rax turned, although Morgan kept his eye on the rancher. In the doorway stood Boose with another man, both loosely cradling shotguns.

"Sorry, Morgan," Boose said. "Business is business. . . ."

"Enough talk!" barked Lardon. "Morgan, Rax—you get out *now* an' don't let me catch you on my land again!"

With that Lardon plucked the cigar from his mouth, stabbed it hard into an earthenware bowl, and scowled as the glowing tip turned dark.

Chapter Seven

Callie, hearing hoofbeats, called, "They're here," and set onto the nightstand the small, wrung-out towel she had been pressing to Clay's forehead. Rising from the chair at his bedside, she moved to the front room even as boots sounded on the porch and the door swept open, admitting a cold gust and Floyd Cooke with a second man at his heels.

"Callie," Cooke shouted, "take Doc's coat!"

The tall, thin man behind Cooke, his cold-flushed cheeks red beneath silver-framed glasses, carried a small black leather satchel fastened by worn leather straps and tarnished brass buckles.

Doc McLean nodded shortly. "Callie," he grunted, in short salutation, his normally smiling blue-gray eyes all business now. He gave her his hat and shrugged free of his heavy coat, revealing a flannel shirt which, pulled on hurriedly over his long-johns, had been misbuttoned.

"Gramps—" Callie began.

"This way, Gordon," said Cooke, hurriedly ushering the doctor into his and Lena's bedroom.

In the bed the boy lay unmoving, his face ash-colored. Lena sat on the edge of the mattress beside him, her two withered hands holding his. She didn't look up when the others came in.

"Sorry to come under such circumstances, Lena," said the doctor, moving gently beside her and slipping the small hand from hers to hold it by the wrist. But the medical man held it only a moment before he stiffened, then quickly bent and pressed two fingers to the boy's neck.

"Why, I can barely feel a pulse. Here, let's try some of this . . ."

He brought a small brown bottle from his bag, pulled its stopper, and held the smelling salts beneath the boy's nostrils.

"Nothing," McLean said.

After a moment, McLean slowly straightened, looking at Lena still on the edge of the bed.

"He's in a coma," said the doctor.

"But he'll be all right—say he'll be all right!" Lena pleaded.

From the doorway came a choked gasp. Floyd Cooke moved quickly to his wife's side and put his arm around her. Callie entered behind him. Gently the doctor set the boy's hand down.

"I'm as sorry as can be," McLean said. "But Lena, I just don't know. He's got his swallow reflex and that means you can feed 'im water and broth to keep his strength up, but whether he'll come out of it—there's just no way to say. I wish I could do more, but all we can do is watch and see."

"We rode as hard as we could!" Floyd Cooke blurted to his wife.

"I know you did," said the old woman. "That wouldn't a mattered. He's been like this since you left. He never woke." She sighed. Lena turned to the doctor. Her eyes seemed tired, a dullness to them as if the spirit had left her. "You best look after Mr. Clay, now, Gordon. He needs your help bad."

In the light of the lanterns Callie had brought to the smaller bedroom the unconscious man lay with a blanket drawn to his chest, although his right arm lay atop the covering. The doctor sat on the edge of the bed, which sagged under the two men's weight.

Lifting Clay's left wrist, the doctor reached with his other hand to Clay's face and raised an eyelid with the ball of his thumb. "Who is he, Floyd?"

"His name's Will Clay," said Cooke. "Poor fella just stopped for the night! If I'd let im keep riding this wouldn't a happened to im!"

"How long's he been like this?" the doctor asked Callie.

"Since we found him," she said.

"No change?"

Callie shook her head.

"And his breathing—how's that been?"

"Good—strong."

The doctor grunted and leaned back. "Well, he's

got a pulse like a bull. But see here?" The doctor touched a finger to the fallen man's neck, held it there, then removed it. "See how long it takes his color to come back? That's smoke poisoning. Kills more than flames ever do and there's not a thing I can do for it. We'll just hope he didn't breathe too much."

He drew back the cover and in the bright glow of the lanterns looked down at the unconscious man's deep chest and wide shoulders. "These burns don't look too bad and I'll check his back in a minute. But about this arm an shoulder . . ."

"I cleaned it the best I could," Callie said.

"I can see that," McLean said. The wound's seriousness showed in full: The collar-bone was fractured, and the shoulder dislocated. McLean had seen many of each kind of injury, common among riders thrown over a horse's head. "A broken clavicle, to start. And damage to the brachial plexus. I'm guessing there's nerve damage. See this swelling? That beam ground ash right into the tissue—into his blood, maybe," said the doctor. "It's a dirty wound." The medical man looked for several minutes more before finally straightening, and shaking his head.

"There's a good chance this arm won't mend—not with that kind of damage. It's all but crushed." The doctor shook his head grimly. "He just may lose the use of it altogether."

"My gosh, Doc!" Cooke exclaimed.

"I've seen enough like this to know, Floyd," McLean said somberly. "But first things first. I'm going to have to reduce the dislocation—pop it back into the socket. That hurts like the devil, so for now it's good he's out. Come on, Floyd, I'll need help on this."

The doctor turned to Floyd's granddaughter.

"Callie, put up some water to boil in the biggest pot you have, would you? Floyd, I'll also need lots of light. Maybe you can bring in all your lanterns? I'm gonna want to clean this open wound to try to keep out infection." He shook his head somberly as his fingers quickly unbuckled and then opened his bag wide, and began setting out instruments. "This is gonna be a long night. . . ."

Floyd Cooke leaned over one of the lanterns, cupped his hand, and blew out the flame. Streaks of red had begun to appear at the window as the sun climbed above the horizon.

"Have a drink with me, Gordon?"

Doc McLean, sitting heavily in a chair in the front room, his sleeves rolled up his forearms, his shirt collar open and wide sweat stains beneath his arms, nodded, exhausted.

"Guess I will, Floyd. Thanks."

From the cupboard Cooke removed two glasses, then reached to the top shelf for a tall, brown, tightly corked bottle.

Cooke poured a couple of fingers' worth into the glasses and the two men drank.

Lena and Callie had gone back to the big bedroom to attend to the boy, while Clay lay in the boy's bed.

"Has he got people to notify?" McLean asked.

"No one," said Cooke. "It's just him."

"Well, he shouldn't be moved for a good week, at least. After that I guess we can bring him in my buckboard to my place."

Cooke put a hand on McLean's arm. "If it's all right with you, Gordon, I think we'd as soon keep him here."

The doctor looked at him.

"He was tryin' to save our boy," Cooke said. "He didn't have to, but he did. We owe him. Yeah, we'll keep him here if you tell us what to do for him."

McLean nodded. "I'll keep stopping in, but there's nothing I can do for him that you can't, and if we can avoid moving him, all the better." McLean reached for his bag.

"All right. First, here's something to help him sleep," he said, bringing out a blue bottle. "Two teaspoons four times a day." Next came a green bottle. "Tincture of opium for the pain. A tablespoon when it gets bad. Be sure to keep an eye on the wound. If it gets infected, it'll raise a fever, and you'll want to knock it down with cool compresses. I'll come back out in a day or so to keep an eye out for signs of gangrene, but meanwhile change the dressings three or four times . . ."

"Thanks, doc."

Callie came in from the other room. She closed the door.

"How's your gran'mom?" Cooke asked.

Callie took the old man's arm. "She's resting." She looked at the doctor. "How will he be, Doc?"

"Too soon to tell, Callie. I've explained to your

grandad about tending the wound, but there's also the burns to consider. Floyd, here's one last medicine, some ointment.'' McLean brought out a bottle with a black rubber squeeze-ball at the top attached to what looked like a small metal funnel. ''Spray this on his back, the bottom of his feet—wherever he's burned. It smells bad, but it'll soothe him.''

''Preciate it, Gordon.''

''And you'll need to keep him warm; skin keeps warmth and body fluids in, an bad burns interfere with the skin's ability to do either. So give him fluids an keep him warm.''

The doctor closed and buckled his bag, accepted his coat and hat, and prepared to leave.

Cooke shook his hand. ''Thanks, Gordon.''

Callie put her arm around the old man's shoulders.

McLean sighed deeply. ''You tell Lena again I'm sorry about the boy, Floyd.''

And with that the doctor left.

Chapter Eight

The days passed in a haze as Clay slipped into and out of consciousness. Sun up . . . sun down . . . No sooner did he wake than he drifted off again, unsure, in his fevered state, of the time, day, or even where he was. Only the throbbing at his shoulder, the trembling of his sweating body and the bedclothes hot and damp beneath him were real. Often he dreamed he was in the barn again—his face to the ground, his lungs scorched, the crushing loft beam clamping his arm as flames licked his skin. He woke from these nightmares lurching in bed, sweat-soaked. But always his eyelids felt immediately leaden again, impossible to hold open, and he drifted off the next moment.

Nonetheless, events punctuated the passing time. Occasionally he woke to the touch of strong fingers at his wrist. Moments later they began prodding his aching shoulder or tapping his chest as the cold cone of a stethoscope pressed above his heart. A man's voice accompanied these acts, sounding deep and serious, yet kindly in tone, speaking apparently to others nearby although to Clay the words remained too distant to understand.

Other times Clay felt something cool pressed to his burning forehead. He opened his eyes to find Callie sitting close on the edge of the bed, her clear green eyes studying him as she wiped his brow with a moist cloth. Though when she saw him awake her lips moved, her murmured words—like the doctor's—remained indecipherable. And several times Clay woke to find the room bathed in moonlight. Blinking, he discerned Callie in a rocking chair beside the bed, her head back, eyes gently closed, breath even, the compress loosely in her hand dangling off the arm of the chair.

And then one day Clay dreamed someone was cutting him, piercing his throbbing arm. Half awake, he reached for it, but in the darkness—was the moon down, or cloud-covered, or were the window curtains just drawn?—he couldn't find his right arm or hand with his left. Groping, he felt only bandages. He blinked, confused. Fighting a swirling dizziness, he struggled from bed. Did he fall? He didn't know, but suddenly hands were upon him, several pairs guiding him back, accompanied by urgent voices: ". . . need to rest . . . been through a lot . . . regain your strength . . ." He resisted. He had questions, important questions he needed answered, but he left off struggling when he recognized Callie's voice and felt her smooth hands cool on his bare left shoulder. He settled down again into a drugged sleep.

In this way two, three, and finally four days passed, until one morning Clay opened his eyes and could tolerate the light. Callie sat at his bedside.

"Your fever's broken," she said. "The worst is over."

And now Clay could taste the warm and flavorful broth Callie spooned for him, and could hear her speak of the strength it would give him. Days and nights became separate from one other, and Callie came at regular intervals, bringing him fresh-baked corn bread. Clay said little. Callie accepted this and did not press him to talk. "I know," she said one afternoon, pausing as she carried away dishes. "You have a lot to think about now. You can talk when you're ready, there's no rush."

One day Floyd Cooke stood at Clay's bedside. "The doc'll be here this afternoon," he said. He studied Clay. "You look better."

"I don't remember gettin' outta the barn," Clay said.

"We pulled you out," said Cooke. "Tied wet towels across't our faces an' dragged you."

Clay nodded. For some days he had known he lay in the boy's room, in his bed, yet had seen no sign of him. "And Danny?"

The old man sat heavily on the corner of the bed and looked at the floor. "Our Danny's in a coma.

Doc says he doesn't know when he'll come out—or *if* he'll come out. We've got him in Cal's room where she can keep an eye on him."

Clay sighed deeply and shook his head.

Cooke seemed to study the spotted backs of his hands on his knees. "Doc says he breathed too much smoke—or maybe it was that crack on his head, probably from the beam that hit you." Cooke sighed deeply. "He must'a gone to check on the colt. Maybe set the lantern too near the hay an' fell asleep."

Clay suddenly remembered his warning to the boy: *Hang the lantern on a nail. Be careful of the hay!* So easy for a boy to forget, though.

"Yup," Cooke continued, "probably he woke up, saw the fire, thought he'd catch all heck for it an' figured to put it out hisself." Cooke wagged his head and chuckled quietly. "By the time he knew he needed help, he'd got all turned around in the smoke."

Clay looked up fiercely. "I could have stopped him."

Cooke raised his eyes.

"He woke me," Clay continued. "He was climbin' out the window with blankets for the colt an' I saw him—talked to 'im!"

"Clay—"

"I told 'im not to be out long. . . . I could've stopped him!"

"*Clay.*" Cooke lay a hand on Clay's forearm. "Don't do this. Don't blame yourself. You couldn't a knowed what would happen. You ran in to *save* him."

"But *didn't!*" Clay snapped.

"But did all you could—more than most men would've. You ain't to blame. We're obliged to you."

Clay shook his head.

"You did your best," the older man continued. "That's all it's fair to ask of any man."

A horse's hooves and the wheels of a buggy sounded then, and Cooke looked toward the window. "That'll be the doc." He rose and went out.

Doc McLean's big hands moved gently over Clay's arm. "Can you feel this? How about this? . . . Turn your head away now an' tell me, can you can feel . . . this?"

Clay's response never changed: "Nothin'. . . . No. . . . Nothin'. . . ."

"Mmm," the doctor said, finally straightening beside the bed.

"Well?" Clay asked. "How long before I can use it again? *Feel* it again?"

The doctor cleared his throat. "First off, know you're lucky to be alive. Between the fire, smoke, an' fallin' timber—not to mention the infection of those first few days—most men wouldn't be lyin' here now."

Clay watched the medical man.

"You're strong," the doctor went on, "or maybe just stubborn. Either way, I'm surprised you're still alive."

"It ain't gonna heal," Clay said. "That's what you're tryin' to say. You can't do anything for it and it's gonna stay like this.'' He looked at the doctor levelly.

McLean met Clay's gaze, and took the measure of the man. ''There's terrible nerve damage,'' the doctor said.

''By all rights the bone should've been shattered. It would've been, if the beam had caught it any different. But the muscle and nerves are still badly compressed.''

''No chance at all then?''

The medicine man hesitated.

''No chance at all I'll use it again?'' Clay asked.

The doctor shook his head. ''Sometimes nerve channels do reestablish themselves. It starts with a tingling, like when your foot's asleep and wakes up. That'd be a good sign. But this kind of injury—well, odds are a thousand to one against it. There's still so much medicine doesn't know—like with young Danny.''

Clay looked off out the window.

''I know it's hard news to hear,'' the doctor said. He sighed, turned to his bag, snapped it closed. ''It's hard news to give, too. But believe it or not, things'll look better. Just give 'em time.''

McLean went out. Clay heard his voice in the other room, and after a while the horse pulled the carriage away.

Lucky, Clay thought. He didn't feel lucky. He used to say that anything that left him his two hands and his legs to walk away on he could survive. Where did that leave him now? Where would he go? How would he live? A flail-armed cripple! Cattle drives?

No one would hire him. He remembered a feedstore man years ago. A store clerk. The man had had a dead arm, and though he sold goods and tallied sums, he never carried items out to the wagons. Would that be Clay one day? He'd always taken pride in his strength, his independence. And now?

What had he done to deserve this? Nothing he could think of. Just stopped to spend the night. And tried to save the boy—who might never wake again!

First Rachel, now this.

He spent the rest of the day staring out the window. When Callie tapped at the door asking if he were ready to eat, he told her no. She returned several times, but each time his answer was the same. He watched the sky go from blue to pink to black.

Chapter Nine

Clay opened his eyes and lay listening in the darkness. There had been a noise. He didn't know what time it was, but sensed it was late, hours to sunrise. His shoulder pained him, but not so badly he couldn't have drifted off again had he not continued to listen. It sounded again, from the other room, and this time he recognized it: a woman weeping. *Callie*. Obviously she was trying to be as quiet as possible, but her muffled sobs still found Clay. He pictured her at the kitchen table, head bent, sleeve pressed to her eyes.

As the sobs continued—muffled, but deep and wracking, showing the depth of her pain—Clay felt surprised. This was the first slip he had seen in the brave face she had worn since the fire. But of course it made sense that such a fine, sensitive girl should be so pained by the week's events. And the face she had been wearing? Nothing more than that: a face, a pose, to conceal her suffering. Clay felt suddenly ashamed. He had been so swept up by his own pain and loss, he had failed to think of anyone else's. True, his loss was terrible, but had not these good people suffered, too?

Clay clenched his fist.

That he had been so mindlessly selfish wasn't the worst of it. If only he could do something for them now, he might make amends—begin to repay them. But do what? Not bring Danny back to them, of course, nor replace the lost stock, but rebuild the barn? At one time this, at least, would have been within his power, by the sweat of his brow. He had always been handy with tools.

But now?

Clay looked at his bandages, pale in the moonlight. He had been active all his life, physically more than capable. Yet now with but one arm, what good was he? Best to face it: He was a cripple.

He wanted to apologize to Callie, to say he was sorry for only taking, never giving, and wondered, *should I to speak with her now?* But then he heard a chair scrape and floorboards creak, and after a moment the old peoples' bedroom door softly closed and its latch clicked. Then all grew quiet.

Clay lay fully awake. He turned to the window and gazed at the sky, a deep blue frosted with stars. Never before had he spent so much time thinking! Always there had been cattle to work, horses to break, fences and roofs to mend. For years this had been his way, working from sunrise to evening, then collapsing each night into an exhausted, dreamless sleep. But these past weeks. . . . How much he had been *thinking*. It was from lying abed, of course: Even while recuperating a man could sleep only so much, then he must lie awake, just him and his thoughts. It occurred to Clay that perhaps for a long time he hadn't *wanted* to think because thoughts turned inevitably to memories, and memories turned to Rachel. And now not just the anguish of losing her plagued him, but despair, because in a world where women died young and infants perished—and accidental fires ruined young boys' lives, old men's livelihoods and stole a grown man the use of his arm—could a man really deny his ultimate powerlessness in the face of so much injustice?

Clay blinked as the sun's first rays slipped above the sash. The sky had gone rose-colored. He watched the beginning of a new day—a day that for him, like each one now for the rest of his life, would find him no more than half a man.

Chapter Ten

Clay opened his eyes to the light of late morning filtering through the window curtains. He had fallen into a fitful sleep around daybreak at last, and someone, doubtless Callie, had closed the curtains to let him continue what she must have imagined a restful sleep. From the kitchen came sounds of quiet activity—a cupboard door squeaking, the tread of a foot, murmured voices.

Gazing at the blue-patterned curtain fabric aglow with the morning sun, Clay still felt troubled about the previous night. Hearing Callie had brought home how selfish he had been acting, and after his shame had come feelings of helplessness, rage, and frustration. Well, this lying abed wasn't helping. He was unused to spending time indoors—let alone on his back—having not done so in years, not since his last stint deputying. In those days when he'd worn a gun on each hip, he'd walked into a bank one morning to find three men with drawn pistols shouting orders at the clerks. He'd stopped that robbery, leaving two men dead on the bank floor and the third to die in the doctor's office that night, but in the crossfire caught two .45 slugs himself. Both had passed between his ribs and out his back—one shattered a picture window, the other thwacked into a heavy oak door—but he'd been bedridden for three weeks. Since then Clay hadn't spent more than a day at a time indoors and doing so now made him miserable. He must get out of this prison of a bed, and out of this room, so crowded with his thoughts.

He sat up, swung his legs over the edge of the mattress, and immediately felt the pain flare from collarbone to ribs along his right side. But it was no longer the agonizing knife-twist of prior days, now it was more a dull, burning ache. Grimacing, he drew a deep breath. He'd always been a speedy healer, recovering from countless injuries through the years quickly, and only hoped his body wouldn't fail him now. His eyes flicked to the small brown bottle on the bureau. He would keep the painkiller near, but use it sparingly.

Standing, he turned to the chair in the corner. Weeks ago he had placed his clothes on it haphazardly, yet now they lay neatly folded. No doubt more of Callie's work. Seeing his boots side by side, Clay mused, *Had so much time really passed since I'd last worn them? How a man's life could change. . . .* He managed to pull on his trousers, then, catching sight of his reflection in the mirror above the bureau, he paused.

His face looked leaner now, the familiar creases at either side of his mouth cutting deeper. But the jaw Rachel called oversized and the blue-gray eyes she likened to bits of stream pebble seemed the same. And his arm—what would Rachel have said about it? Probably that he was a better man with one good one than most men were with two. Something like that. Clay caught himself still seeing through her eyes. Would he do so always? He didn't know.

His right arm hung heavily at his side, a useless thing. He tried to raise it but felt nothing. Grasping the wrist with his left hand, he watched the hand hang, as limp and heavy as a dead man's. What to do with it? Picking up his shirt, he worked the sleeve up around his bad arm, pinched it to his shoulder with his chin—he ignored the pain at his collarbone—then reached awkwardly back, struggling to get his left arm through. Finally he moved to tie the right arm across his chest using a sling he fashioned from his bandanna. It took him some time, but at length he was done. Sweeping his hair from his forehead, which was damp from his effort and pain, he sat in the chair, pulled on his boots, then headed for the door.

Seeing Clay standing in the doorway, Lena said, "You're up!" She straightened with effort from where she had been wiping the table.

Callie turned sharply from the cabinets. "Will, you shouldn't be out of bed yet! How do you feel?"

He shook his head. "Like I'll go crazy if I lie there another minute."

"Well, that sounds like a good sign," Lena said. "Callie, pour Will some coffee."

Outside, the morning was brisk. Clay moved to the pump stiffly, the ground jolting his heels as if his legs had forgotten their length. At the pump he levered the heavy, iron handle and for a moment watched the sparkling water splash from the spigot. With a start he realized he couldn't both pump and scoop water to his face at the same time, and without hesitation he bent to the icy stream and plunged his head beneath it. The chilling water bit his skin and he whipped upright, gasping and blinking hard. The world looked somehow brand-new, and, feeling the icy rivulets down his neck, he peered toward the mountains. Standing purple-hued and distant, they looked the same as a month ago, and for some reason he found the sight comforting. His gaze shifted toward what had been the barn, now little more than a blackened heap of burned planks and charred beams collapsed in on themselves at odd angles; when the wind shifted, Clay caught a whiff of scorched wood, burnt hay and, beneath it, the unmistakable odor of singed fur. He sighed and looked away and saw a lone figure sitting beneath the big birch.

Floyd Cooke looked up as Clay approached. Sitting on a log, his bony knees spread, his thin forearms on his thighs and his hat dangling from his hands, he had been staring at the tree.

"How do you feel?" he asked Clay.

"Better," Clay said.

Cooke nodded, then sighed at the birch. "He loved to climb this tree. Sometimes wouldn't come down even for dinner."

"It's a good place to sit, then," Clay said.

Both men were quiet for some time. Finally Cooke spoke. "The old woman's taking it hard. Callie's young and strong, she seems all right and I'm thankful. But Lena. . . ." He shook his head.

To Clay, it was all too plain that the ordeal had taken its toll on the old man, too. These past weeks Cooke seemed to have aged years. His spryness and energy were gone, his eyes shone lackluster, and he moved slowly.

"I'm ridin' out to Lardon's today," the old man announced. He squinted toward the mountains. "Gonna tell 'im I'll sell."

"Isn't there any other way?" Clay asked grimly.

The old man shrugged tiredly. "Stock's practically gone, we got no money to rebuild. . . ." He paused, sighed deeply, then raised a hand to run trembling fingers through his thinning white hair. "Anyway, with Danny like this, it somehow don't seem to matter."

"Well, I'd like to ride with you," Clay said after a moment. "If it's all right."

Cooke looked at him appreciatively. "You don't need to, Clay, though I'm beholden for the offer. It's a good couple hours' ride and might be too much for you so soon."

Clay shook his head. "I'd like to, Floyd."

Cooke looked at him and nodded.

* * *

While Cooke changed into heavier clothes, Clay waited with the Appaloosa in front of the shack. When the door opened he was surprised to see Callie, holding a small wicker basket.

"Clay, I thought I might sew that bandanna for you," she said, glancing at his sleeve. "That knot'll probably get uncomfortable."

He looked at her. "You think it's better that way?"

She nodded.

He hesitated, then ducked his head. "Sure, Callie."

She brought a needle and spool of thread from the basket and began to work. She stood close, and Clay could smell the freshness of her hair. At length he said, "I heard you last night."

She paused, and looked at him uncertainly. "Heard me?"

"In the kitchen."

She was quiet. "I'm sorry I woke you, Will."

"Callie, don't apologize—if anyone should be sorry, it's me! The trouble I've put you all to—"

"Will," Callie said suddenly. "Promise you won't tell gramps and grandmom you heard me."

Clay looked at her quizzically.

Callie glanced toward the cabin door. "It's all been so hard on them already, if they knew how I was feeling, it would only hurt them worse."

Clay stared at the young woman. She was so selfless, so caring, he felt torn. On one hand he'd have liked to follow her example—to forget about his own pain, and help this family that had so helped him—but on the other he realized it was precisely his injury that left him powerless to do anything for them. "I . . . I won't say anything, Callie. I just wish there was something I could do for them. . . . Do for *you*—"

The front door creaked and they both turned. Floyd Cooke came out, adjusting his hat. "About ready, Clay?"

Clay turned to Callie.

She smiled. Bending her head, she snapped the thread with her teeth. He looked down at the sleeve, folded and sewn neatly against his side. He looked up at her, and their eyes held. Then Clay turned to the old man.

"Ready, Floyd," he said.

Chapter Eleven

The sun had climbed to its noontime position as Clay and his older riding companion crossed the flatlands of Brack Lardon's property. The sky was a clear, brilliant blue, and the sun beat down warm on Clay's skin. Clay breathed deeply of the clear, fresh air.

"How you holdin' up?" Cooke asked.

Clay nodded. "Good." Then, seeing the old man still looking at him, Clay said, "Really, I'm okay. It hurts a mite, but not bad." He squinted ahead. "How'd he get so much for himself, anyway?"

Cooke shook his head, scowling. "Practically stole it, if you want the truth. Did it all borderline legal, pressing folks to sell when the common stream run dry. Then when Bob Wills died last year and his wife Sally was near off her head grievin', Lardon came to her with the perfect timing of a rattler an' offered her more money than she could say no to. She just wanted to get back East where she had family, and she said yes before thinkin' twice. Once Lardon got that parcel, he could make things hard for the rest of us.'' Cooke turned and spat, then sat up and nodded ahead.

''Here we are now, coming up on 'er just over the ridge . . .''

As the two crested the rise, Clay saw a formidable settlement. A large whitewashed ranch house stood flanked by a sizeable barn, two corrals, and a pair of buildings Clay recognized as a bunkhouse and grub-house. From the size of these last two Clay guessed they might accommodate twenty or so men.

As they rode in through the gate, passing beneath a crossbar with Lardon's brand carved into it—a big B over a big L—Clay became aware of a metal ringing sound at pulselike intervals. His eyes found the open shed where a blacksmith in leather apron stood working at an anvil, his arm rising and falling regularly, the hammer bouncing high after each strike and the sound reaching Clay's ears a moment after each blow.

''Let's check the house, first,'' Cooke said.

They rode across the wide yard, earning long stares from several men, including a tall, thin ranch hand leading a pair of saddled horses toward the barn, and from the blacksmith, who paused in his work to see them to the house. On the porch sat a man with his chair tipped back against the house. He wore a faded yellow plaid shirt, and had watched them ride in without looking away. When they got within a hundred yards, he slowly tipped the chair forward and stood, pulled the brim of his hat low, and moved to the door—watching them all the while. He opened it, and disappeared inside.

Clay noticed that more than a few men wore Mexican-style ponchos across their shoulders, although the men didn't look Mexican. "Lots of Mexican-wear here," he said. "Surprising, this far north."

Cooke said, "Lardon's got a partner of sorts travels up from down that way often. Brings back horses. I wouldn't be surprised if they rustle 'em across the border. Anyway, they bring Mexican clothes and gear, too, cheap. Lardon's crew are the only ones around that wear 'em."

At the big house they reined in and dismounted, tying their animals to the rail. The man in the yellow shirt now reappeared, stepping out of the house slowly, almost lazily, although Clay could see a watchfulness and power to him that reminded Clay of a fighter's poise and balance. He was solidly built, with a thickness and heaviness of shoulder, and forearms dark from the sun. He wore dusty pointed boots, and Clay noticed he wore a gun, holster lashed above his knee with a length of knotted rawhide. Stepping forward on the porch and raising a booted foot to the chair, the man said nothing but just squinted at them, his face remaining half in shadow. Clay saw an unshaved jaw and the trace of a sneer.

"We're here to see Lardon," said Cooke.

The man took his time answering. He moved his

mouth around a plug of tobacco, then turned slightly, keeping his eyes on the men before him, to spit on the dusty floorboards.

"You're Cooke," he said. "I seen you. But who's this here?" He squinted sizing Clay up, his cold eyes finally resting on Clay's shoulder.

"The name's Clay," Clay said, returning the other man's look.

The man on the porch grinned, his mouth twisting wryly. "Get your hand caught in somebody's cookie jar, Clay?"

"We're here to see your boss," Cooke repeated rather quickly.

The man in the doorway bristled. He seemed not to like being reminded he took orders. His eyes grew harder yet and, as he turned, he said, "Come on then." He went in, leaving the door open.

Inside the house, Clay and Cooke walked along shining oak floors. Clay saw the mounted heads of deer, puma, bear, and a moose.

"Likes to kill, don't he?" Clay observed.

Also on the walls hung brightly colored Mexican blankets, with vases and jars on shelves. At a door at the end of the hall the yellow-shirted man knocked. A voice on the other side grunted and the yellow-shirted man opened it. He stepped aside barely enough for Cooke and Clay to pass, then remained leaning against the doorframe as another man came from somewhere in the house to join him.

To Clay, the man behind the desk—not very tall but built burly, with hard eyes under thick, low brows and a cigar clamped between his jaws—looked angry, but also somehow nervous. The man's mouth seemed grim but his eyes shifted watchfully between his visitors. It was the manner of a man slightly nervous, and considering the circumstances it surprised Clay.

"Cooke," the landowner said, nodding grimly, as he eyed Clay. "Who's this with you?"

"A friend," the old man replied.

"The name's Clay," Clay said.

Clay felt the rancher peer at him appraisingly before returning his gaze finally to the old man.

"Well, sit down—both you," Lardon said, motioning, as he settled back into his own chair.

Cooke said, "I'll stand. We been sittin' all morning." He held his hat at his side. "Lardon, I'll get right to the point. I'm here to take up your offer. I'm going to let you buy my place. I don't want to leave, but I got no choice."

Brack Lardon slowly rolled the cigar in his mouth and squinted. He removed the stogie, looked at it as if becoming aware of it only now, and reached for a box of matches on the desk. He struck one and as he held the flame at the end to relight it, alternately sucking and puffing, the thick blue-gray clouds rose toward the ceiling. Clay knew the activity was to stall for time. It tipped Clay off that the man thought himself on sensitive ground. But considering Lardon held all the aces, Clay didn't understand the gesture.

"I had some bad luck out at my place," Cooke grimly continued. "You prob'ly heard. M'grandson, he's . . . he's in a coma. We had a barn fire he got caught in."

"I heard," Lardon said flatly.

"It means we got to leave," the old man went on. "So I'm here to take up your offer."

Lardon studied the cigar tip. "Well, I think we can do business." He took out a pen, paper, and an ink-well from a drawer. "I can draw up a bill a sale we can sign in front a witnesses right now, an' you as good as got the money in your pocket. All we gotta do is come up with a figure."

Cooke seemed startled. "But we already got one.

"Oh, now, easy," Lardon said, smiling and raising his palm. "That was for the whole spread—lock, stock, an' barrel. But the stock's gone now, an' the barn, too. Your principal's been considerably reduced."

"But it's the land you want—we both know that."

"Listen, Cooke, what do you say to eight hundred dollars even? I shouldn't offer you even that much 'cept, well, like I said, I heard about your grandson."

"But you're robbin' me!" the old man blurted.

Lardon's eyes winked in amusement and he gazed toward the doorway.

"Sound like anybody's gettin' robbed to you, Boose? Or you, Shank?" The yellow-shirted man just grinned, but the other shook his head decisively. "No, *sir!*"

Lardon shrugged and his eyes returned to Floyd Cooke. "You should'a took my first offer 'stead a bein' greedy. You got only yourself to blame now."

Clay heard a snort of amusement behind him.

"You're takin' advantage of the man, Lardon," Clay said. "He's got hurt kin, he's bein' forced to leave when he don't want to, an' now you're offerin' a price way below fair value.''

Lardon turned to Clay. ''Cowboy, I don't remember askin' your opinion. This is between me an' Cooke. Why don't you mind your business?''

''Dang right,'' grunted Boose.

Clay felt his anger swell. The rage he had felt while abed these past weeks, in constant pain and wanting nothing more than an enemy, a target for the injustice of the accident, made him glare at Brack Lardon with a cool, white fury.

A hand touched Clay's shoulder. ''Clay, I appreciate your interest,'' Cooke said, ''and I take kindly to your concern. But he's right, this ain't your battle. And anyway,'' the old man turned, and looked the rancher in the eye, ''I ain't takin' up that offer.''

''Think it over,'' Lardon said. ''Take a day or two. Hey, take three or four—as long as you like.''

''Let's go, Clay,'' said Cooke. And to Lardon he said, ''You can go to the devil before I give you my farm for eight hundred dollars.''

''Just don't wait too long,'' Lardon said. ''I'm bein' generous already, an' the offer could always drop.''

Clay and Cooke turned toward the door. Clay caught Boose's eye, and saw the man was still grinning.

''Somethin' funny here?'' Clay said.

Boose stopped smiling and his eyes became razors. He opened his mouth but before he could speak Cooke, close behind Clay, said, ''Come on, Clay, let's go,'' and pressed his young companion forward.

Moments later, in the brightness of the sun, Clay and Cooke stood unhitching their horses. Boose and the other had followed them out and stood watching from the porch as Clay and his friend mounted up, turned their horses, and rode toward the gate.

Chapter Twelve

The ride back was mostly quiet. Clay took his cue from the old man, who seemed uninterested in talking, answering Clay's several attempts at conversation with replies of but a word or two. Clay backed off and left his companion to his thoughts.

As they approached the Cooke settlement, though, Clay noticed the old man's spirit seem to sink even lower. The remains of the barn, which from the distance had appeared a mere blot on the landscape, grew to a charred hulking shell as the riders drew close. To Clay, Cooke's very posture seemed to collapse: His shoulders dropped, his head bowed, and his hands seemed to hold the reins with a weariness Clay hadn't noticed earlier.

Life could be so hard, Clay thought. And suddenly he perceived the common thread in both his and

Cooke's tragedies: In Rachel's death and the baby's, and in what had happened to young Danny, and in Cooke's loss of his farm and Clay's of his arm, there was no one to blame. Fate had delivered her cruel strokes by whim, and if her victims seemed undeserving it proved only how little power men had in their lives. Oh, it might be comforting to believe some grand, overruling scheme duly rewarded the virtuous and punished the evil, as Lena believed, but events dispelled the notion. Decent living? Charity? Innocence? These guaranteed nothing, not fate's favor nor even her mercy. No, Clay decided, if men wanted justice, they would be fools to look to Fate to deliver it.

The two men rode into the corral at last, among the half-dozen cows that had survived. Dismounting and unsaddling their horses, Clay and Cooke rubbed the animals down, then started toward the shack. But Cooke caught Clay's arm.

"This business with Lardon, don't say much about it, Clay. . . . We got to act strong for the women's sake."

Clay nodded, surprised.

As the men came through the cabin door, Callie said, "Good, you're back!"

Cooke nodded tiredly. "Where's your grandmom, Cal?"

Callie pulled out a chair for her grandfather, who accepted it wearily.

"She's lying down," the young woman said.

Cooke shook his head. "In forty-odd years, I've never known that woman to rest before sundown."

"Here, Granddad," said Callie, setting a cup of steaming coffee before Cooke. "And for you, too, Will."

The bedroom door opened. Lena stood with a shawl around her shoulders. "I thought I heard voices."

"How you feelin', dear?" asked Cooke, noticing his wife's paleness as she slowly walked in.

"I'm . . . I'm all right . . . I only lay down for a minute, but I guess I dozed off." She looked at her granddaughter. "Callie, did you cook dinner by yourself?"

"It's stew, Gram, it was nothing." Callie checked the pot over the fire. "It'll be ready soon."

Lena turned to her husband. "Floyd, did you talk with Lardon?"

Cooke nodded shortly. "He's still willing to buy."

"Well, that's something, at least," Lena replied. But then she looked closer at her husband's face. "And he'll pay what he offered before?"

Cooked avoided her eyes. "Well, pretty near. . . ."

"Oh, Floyd!" Lena said. "He's offering less? Even less than before?"

"Gramps!" Callie exclaimed.

Cooke shrugged wearily. "He says the spread's worth less now, so he's offerin' less. The fact is, he's right."

Callie's eyes flashed. "That man's shameless!"

"What are we going to do?" asked Lena.

"Well," said Cooke. "It's plain we can't stay. Not without money or stock."

Callie came to her grandfather's side, pulled out a

chair and sat beside him, and clasped his hands. "But Gramps, after all the work you've put in—and you both here so long!"

"I don't know," Cooke said. "I guess we can always go back East."

"Back East!" Callie exclaimed. "But you hated it there! People living on top of one another, all the noise. . . . You've always said how much you love this land!" She turned to her grandmother. "You've said so, too, Gram. . . . And what would we do there?"

"I don't know!" Cooke said. "I just don't know! But our backs are against the wall!" Suddenly he stood and spun toward the coat pegs. "I'm . . . I'm goin' to the barn. There's things—things I can salvage. The plough, tools . . . Things to take with us . . ."

"Oh, Floyd," said Lena, her tone immediately softer. "You don't need to do that this minute, do you, dear? The food will be ready soon."

But Cooke didn't look her way. "No, I . . . I'll be in soon. I just want to . . . make a start. . . ."

With that he took his coat and hat and went out. Lena looked after him. Clay and Callie exchanged a look, then Clay moved to the coat pegs, too. "I'll be in soon," he said.

Stepping onto the porch as he shrugged into his jacket, Clay called, "Floyd?" Halfway toward the barn, the old man turned. "I'll give you a hand," Clay said, and joined the old man, who stood waiting with his hands dug in his pockets.

At the barn, little more than two sections of adjoining walls still stood connected by a piece of sagging roof. Amid the heavy, acrid smell inside blackened beams lay pointing in all directions.

"It's an awful sight," said Cooke. "I built 'er myself when we first came out. The men that helped—most are dead or have left the territory." He shook his head. "Now this is gone, too. . . . Well, what's left a the plow should be over that way," he said, pointing.

Bits of charcoal squeaked underfoot as they made their way amid the ruins, steadying themselves by grabbing ends of charred beam that often snapped loose in their hands and blackened their palms. Cooke tried to move a six-foot length of roof beam, but couldn't manage.

"Here, let me help," said Clay. Together they shoved the beam aside. Cooke bent and brushed ash from the blackened plow blade, whose handles had burned completely away.

"There'll be a log splitter an' sledge, too," he said. "In back there." Clay followed that way.

Near the rear of the wreckage, Cooke suddenly stopped. He put out a hand and touched the blackened remains of a crumbling gate. "The colt's stall!" he said. "Danny was so happy. . . . He loved that little fella. Another year an' he'd a been ridin' 'im!" Suddenly the old man clutched the charred post and bowed his head. Clay reached quickly to steady him.

"He's just a boy!" Cooke blurted. "Why'd it have to happen to *him?* Why not *me?* I've had my time. Danny has his whole life ahead."

"Floyd, let's head back. You've got to be tired an' you can lie down."

"But the sledge . . . we got to get it."

"There's time later. Come on."

Floyd let Clay help him out, the old man leaning on Clay as Clay put his arm beneath the older man.

"Listen, Clay, I'm sorry. I just saw where the colt was an'. . . . Yeah, I've got to lie down. . . ."

When they came in the door, Callie exclaimed, "Grandpa!" Lena came quickly from the small room, holding a lantern. "Floyd?" said the old woman. "What's wrong?" and she rushed to his side.

"He just needs to lie down," said Clay.

"Broke down like a little kid," muttered the old man, shaking his head as they helped him.

Lena and Callie led him to the other room. "Easy now, Gramps."

"There, now, Floyd," said Lena. "You lie down a while. . . ." They helped him to the bedroom, went inside, closed the door.

After a few minutes Callie came out. "He's resting," she said.

"He wanted to find the sledge," said Clay. "But it's probably better if he doesn't go in there again. I'll see if I can find it."

Again inside the barn, Clay returned to the back. Sifting through the debris, he found an ax head and scythe blade, both deeply blackened. He continued to poke and stir through the wreckage, and finally spotted the sledgehammer head lying like a square-edged stone on the ash-gray ground. He picked it up and was making his way back, when, as he shoved aside a section of planking near where the door had been, amid the blackness on the ground a glinting bit of metal caught his eye. He bent and picked up a round, silver dollar–size object, faintly shining, with points around its outer edge. He wiped it on his jeans and recognized it as a spur wheel. A large-size, Mexican-style rowel with a dozen points. Clay looked up. What was it doing here? If it had been lying in the middle of the dirt floor before the fire, Clay would have noticed it. Had it been the boy's? Had he brought it with him with the blankets that night? But for what reason? It made no sense. Clay hadn't seen one of these in years. Or rather, he corrected himself, since this morning. At Lardon's ranch.

And suddenly Clay felt his puzzlement give way to a flicker of suspicion. His mouth grew taut. Hardly daring to admit the forming thought, he began looking around—out of curiosity, he told himself, but with an intensity that belied idle investigation. He lifted some beams, shoved others aside, his eyes sharp. Would there be anything else? No reason to think so. He wasn't even sure what he was looking for, although he knew he would recognize it if he found it. And then, lifting a section of loft flooring near the front door, he saw something crushed and blackened beneath. He bent close and recognized it as a can—once rectangular but now crushed, the kind that held kerosene. Crushed and blackened, to be sure, but a kerosene can without question. Grasping it and straightening up, Clay dimly remembered something Lena had said the night he had arrived.

She had been complaining about the boy's neglecting a chore. . . . Was that it?. . . . Yes, the boy's duty included keeping the lanterns filled, but he hadn't. They had run out, and Danny hadn't set the empty can in the buckboard so Cooke would know to buy more when he rode into town. Lena had had to put the can in the buckboard herself. Clay looked at the can in his hand. *Lena had had to do it herself,* yet here was the can *not in the buckboard at all.* Clay turned toward the far end of the barn. With narrowed eyes, he went scrabbling toward it.

Half-covered by a section of roof which he had to drag aside, the buckboard was now little more than a collapsed, ash-covered heap with four metal wheel rims beside it. Clay rooted through it, raising ashy white dust. And there, beside what had been the seat, he saw what looked like—yes, a blackened can.

Clay slowly lifted it and looked back toward the other can. Where had it come from? And as Clay stared, his mind returned to the night of the fire: He had come running into the barn and caught a barely perceptible, yet unmistakable scent of kerosene.

Someone had been here the night of the fire.

Clay was starting to fit the pieces together. And now he thought of the lantern Lena had just been carrying from the boy's room—the lantern that was supposed to have started the fire!

Clay's eyes narrowed. And all the rage, fury, and frustration of these past weeks suddenly focused. There could be no other explanation. The fire wasn't accidental.

Clay looked at the spur wheel gripped in his hand

and his eyes narrowed. And suddenly Clay had a target—someone to blame.

''Clay?''

It was Callie's voice, calling from the porch. ''Clay, dinner's ready.''

He turned toward the house. Should he tell them that it had been Lardon? That Lardon or his men had burned down the barn—*done that to Danny* . . . No! The old people were already so broken down, who could say what effect this might have?

''Clay?''

But should he tell her? He set the can down and moved toward the house. She stood on the porch, smiling, and he stepped toward her.

''Callie, I've got to leave.''

She looked at him, puzzled. ''But, Will, the food's on the table.'' Then she saw something in his eyes. Her hand reached to catch his sleeve. ''Will, leave to go where? For how long?''

He looked into her eyes. ''Callie, listen. I don't know for how long. I'll be back as soon as I can. Tell your grandparents.'' He turned.

''But Will!'' she said. ''Can't you even tell me where?''

''It's better you don't know. I'll tell you later, but for now there's nothing to gain by your knowing, and it can only hurt. Trust me.''

And with that he saddled up and rode out.

Chapter Thirteen

It was early evening as Clay rode up Sharpton's Main Street. A hardware store, milliner's, lunchroom, and saloon—these and a half dozen other shops lining the street made the town like a thousand dusty others spread across the territory. But none was the storefront Clay sought, and he continued to walk the Appaloosa. As people passed, Clay could feel their curious glances; then, remembering his slinged arm, he wondered if it was the cause of their sidelong looks.

Above a doorway ahead hung a five-pointed wooden star the size of a wagon wheel. Clay rode toward it. Dismounting, he found his shoulder gave him some pain, likely from his hours in the saddle. As he wound the reins around the hitching rail, he read the black lettering on the plate-glass window: RANCE BARTON, SHERIFF, SHARPTON, MONTANA.

Grasping the door handle, Clay went in.

Like most lawmen's offices, the room was cluttered. A chest-high wooden file cabinet stood with half its drawers opened, a wall-mounted rifle rack hung not quite level, and on a corkboard beside a coatrack a dozen sketches of men's faces—the word WANTED above some, REWARD above others—were pinned overlapping each other. Two cells sat in back, one empty, its door ajar, the other with someone asleep on the bunk, his back to the room. As Clay entered a man sitting at the desk, a metal star hung pinned to his shirt, looked up. About forty-five years old, he wore his gray hair short, his mustache trimmed, and had sharp gray eyes. Upon seeing Clay, he scowled.

"I was about to head for supper, stranger. I hope you ain't here about trouble."

Clay unbuttoned his coat. "As a matter of fact, I am."

The sheriff eyed Clay's sleeve. "You must be the fella out at Cooke's place. Doc Mclean mentioned about the fire."

"The name's Clay."

The sheriff nodded. "You say you're here about trouble?" His tone was none too friendly.

Clay set his hat on a chair.

"A few hours ago I was helpin' Cooke sift through what's left of his barn." Clay slipped two fingers into his shirt pocket and drew out the spur rowel. "I found this." He handed it to Barton.

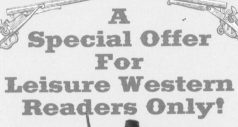

The sheriff studied the wheel in his hand. ''It's Mexican, but you probably know that.''

Clay nodded. ''I also know a lotta Brack Lardon's men wear 'em. They'd be unusual around these parts otherwise, wouldn't you say?''

Barton looked up sharply but before he could speak, the door swung open and a man of perhaps sixty—large, overweight, in a worn-looking suit and string tie—barreled in.

''Rance,'' he said, ''I need those vouchers Friday. I don't want to sit on 'em.''

''Right, Mayor,'' said the sheriff. The man in the suit nodded and began to turn, but then, eyeing the newcomer, he paused.

''You must be the stranger out at Cooke's. I was sorry to hear about the fire. It was a tragedy.''

Clay looked at him. ''Yes, it was.''

''What brings you to town?''

Clay nodded toward the sheriff. ''I found a spur rowel in the ashes of Cooke's barn.''

''Yes?'' the mayor said.

''I was in the barn earlier that night,'' Clay said, ''and if it'd been lying where I found it, I'd have seen it. It wasn't there before the fire.''

''A rowel?'' said the mayor.

Clay nodded toward the wheel, still in the sheriff's hand. ''Like the kind Brack Lardon's ranch hands wear.''

''He thinks Lardon set the fire—or had someone do it,'' Barton said. ''To buy Cooke out.'' The sheriff looked at Clay. ''That about right?''

Clay nodded grimly. ''It is.''

"'Course the youngster was in the barn after you," said the mayor. "He might'a brought it in with him. You know how boys are—he could'a found it anywhere."

Clay looked at him levelly. "I got a different idea."

Barton raised his eyebrows.

"That fire was no accident," Clay said. "It was set."

"Mister, that's a serious charge," the sheriff said.

"Arson's always serious, Sheriff, especially when someone almost dies. Cooke an' his family think the fire started when the boy kicked over a lantern, but the lantern he's supposed to have used is still sittin' on his bedroom dresser—he never brought it out to the barn at all. I realized that later, an' with all they got on their minds, I'm not surprised they haven't noticed. Another thing: When I ran into the barn during the fire, I smelled kerosene. Not strong, just a trace—but it was there. And before the fire I didn't smell any. The old woman even mentioned they were out of kerosene and needed to buy some. Yet I found *two* empty cans. I think Lardon had that fire set to burn Cooke out so he could snatch up his land."

"Mister," said Barton, "I don't like what I'm hearin'."

"Yeah, well what I'd like to know," said Clay, "is why you're so pigheaded set on not believin' me."

"Watch it, now," the sheriff growled. "This is *my* town and I don't like strangers tryin' to ride roughshod over me. An' I'll tell you somethin' else: A man rides in with all kinds a accusations 'gainst one a the most influential men in the territory, I ask myself, what's this fella got to gain?"

"Not a thing," Clay said. " 'Cept to pay back what I owe the Cookes by seein' Lardon gets what's comin' to 'im." Clay's eyes narrowed. "Besides, just maybe I got somethin' of a personal stake in all this."

"Well, if anything sounds rotten to me, it's that the same night you ride in, the Cookes have their fire."

Clay's eyes flashed. "What would I gain by burnin' the man's barn?"

"Good question—an' I'll give it some thought, don't you worry," Barton said.

"An' I suppose I did *this* on purpose, too!" Clay shot back, jerking his thumb toward his shoulder.

Barton tossed the rowel onto the desk.

"All right, men," the mayor interrupted, "easy, now!" He turned to Clay. "Clay, you're makin' serious charges an' they need serious backing. Now I have no idea if what you're saying is true. Lardon's pulled an unpopular deal or two, that's no secret, but something like this? You've gotta have proof."

Clay snatched up the rowel. "What do you call this? And the kerosene cans and the lantern?"

"I call it a start," said the mayor. "But it's all circumstantial evidence. You need more—a witness, say."

Clay scowled bitterly. "The only witness was the boy."

"Or a confession," said the mayor. "Verbal or signed, either would do."

Clay snorted. "If *you* was Lardon, would *you* confess?"

"Well, just know that the circuit judge comes through next month," the mayor said. "And if this is all you give him, he'll throw the case right out."

The sheriff said, "An' I know I'm not about to ride out and accuse Brack Lardon of arson with nothin' more than this."

Clay spun on Barton. "Maybe Lardon's got more influence than some people let on."

Barton shot to his feet. "That's enough, mister! Now you can ride out the way you rode in, or I'll run you in . . . Let you cool your heels in a cell a few nights."

The mayor stepped between the two. "Listen, Clay," he said, putting his arm around Clay's shoulder, "you get some proof—a confession or *something*—an' you'll have a case. But right now you got nothing."

Clay snatched up his hat and angrily turned. "All right. I will. You count on it."

And with that he strode out, yanking the door closed.

Chapter Fourteen

It was growing late in the afternoon, the sun casting long shadows, as Clay jerked the reins from the hitching rail, swung into the saddle, and turned the Appaloosa's head in the direction out of town.

The Mexican spur rowel, the crushed kerosene can, the smell of kerosene in the fire, and the lantern still in the boy's bedroom all combined to give positive proof the blaze had been no accident. Glancing at the sky, Clay realized he wouldn't reach his destination before early evening, but he knew where he must go.

Leaving Sharpton, Clay rode hard, his anger building. When the fire had seemed accidental, he had felt bitter but resigned: If chance alone seemed the root of a tragedy, what more could one do but try to cope? Lying abed feeling helpless, guilty and frustrated,

Clay had been a man without purpose. But now that he knew a person was, or people were, behind this—ones who had plotted and schemed to serve their own ends no matter how high the price—Clay's resolve focused into a sharp, white fury that drove him to act. Riding hard, he wasn't sure what he would do when he reached his destination, but to return to the Cookes—and especially to Callie—having not done anything, no, this wasn't a possibility. The pent-up fury of these past weeks drove him.

It was nearly supper time when Clay reached Brack Lardon's ranch. Few men were about. One led a horse to the barn, and another crossed toward the grub house, but neither took especial interest in Clay. Clay saw that the yellow-shirted man wasn't on the porch now, although his chair still rested near the wall. Dismounting quickly, Clay tied the Appaloosa, and without pausing strode onto the porch. He grasped the door's handle and shoved the door open wide, going in to trace the way he had come yesterday.

At the end of the hall Lardon's door stood open.

Clay strode boldly in. "Lardon, you got some explainin' to do."

Sitting at his desk with the men of yesterday standing before him, Lardon looked up sharply. Boose, having turned, began toward Clay. "Well, hey, pard! Where do you think you're—"

But Lardon silenced his man, barking, "Boose! Leave him be." With his eyes on the newcomer, Lardon said, "It's 'Clay,' ain't it? I don't much like people bargin' into my house, but I guess I know why you're here. Come to accept my offer to the old man, eh?''

Clay stepped to the edge of the desk and, glaring, pulled the spur rowel from his shirt pocket and dropped it onto the middle of the desk.

Lardon stared at the darkened rowel, then frowned at Clay. ''What's this?''

''It's from the pile a burned planks that used to be Cooke's barn,'' Clay said. ''I found it in there yesterday. Your men wear that kind, don't they?''

The ranch owner squinted at Clay, then picked up the rowel and turned it in his fingers. Then he dropped it back on the desk. ''So? What're you gettin' at?''

''I'm getting at a fire that wasn't accidental but deliberate. Set by someone who stood to gain by Cooke leaving.'' Clay leaned forward across the desk. ''I'm getting at a fire set to burn a man out, but that nearly killed a boy—which means attempted murder. Am I bein' clear enough for you, Lardon?''

Lardon looked at him a long moment. Then he reached for his cigar box on the desk, took his time snipping the end of one, and lighted it. Finally he grinned—slowly, as much a sneer as anything else.

''I hear lots of accusations,'' he said, ''but not a word of anything concrete. If you're so sure, why not go to the sheriff?''

Clay's eyes narrowed. ''I've just come from Rance Barton. You got 'im sewed up in your pocket, haven't you?''

Lardon laughed. ''Sounds to me like you got

nothin', then, cowboy. Some far-fetched ideas, but not a stitch a proof.''

Boose snickered.

''Now, listen,'' Lardon continued, ''why don't you run along, Clay. An' tell Cooke not to wait too long to take up my offer—it won't stand forever.'' He bent his to his paperwork.

Clay snatched up the spur wheel and with his forearm swept the desk clear, scattering papers, pen, and inkwell across the floor. With a muttered curse Boose started forward, but Lardon again barked a command to restrain him.

''All right, Clay, get out!'' Lardon ordered. ''An' when you can prove something—*then* you show your face here again!''

''Count on it, Lardon!'' Clay shot back. And with that he spun toward the door, shouldering roughly past the two men.

Chapter Fifteen

As Clay burst onto the porch, bouncing the front door on its hinges, the setting sun's rays stabbed at his eyes. For a moment he stood breathing hard, squinting at the mountains; a knot of muscle at the back of his neck was bunched like a fist. He became aware of a stinging sensation in his hand and looked down to see blood; he was clutching the spur rowel tightly enough for its points to have pierced his palm. Scowling, he shoved the wheel into his pocket and wiped his palm on the leg of his jeans.

Well, he hadn't accomplished a thing. He had let his bottled-up rage of these past weeks lead him, driving him here to make accusations he could not support, and he'd accomplished nothing useful at all. He felt disgusted.

A few yards away two men stood at the rail, their

horses at the watering trough. The men wore dusty shirts, worn jeans, and scuffed boots. They had glanced at Clay when he burst through the door, their eyes flicking to him curiously, but then they returned to their conversation.

"Yeah," said the taller man, "that sneaky polecat took me, all right."

"How much you say?" asked the other man.

"Two dollars."

The second man cocked an eye. "An' you think he left 'cause a *that*?"

"Why else? Man ups and leaves sudden. . . . Listen, always watch a fella owes you poker money. Nine times outta ten he'll try to skip out."

"But payday ain't 'til Friday," persisted the other man. "It don't make sense he'd leave 'fore wages just to keep your two dollars."

Clay had started to unwind the Appaloosa's reins from the rail, but, despite his disgust, he found himself listening.

"Well, who knows—he probably owed other fellas money, too."

"Well, could be. . . . Say, that fight with Peely last week? He'd like to've beat 'im to death if people hadn't pulled 'im off. Listen, it's worth two dollars to have him gone."

"Easy for you to say—ain't your two dollars."

Clay turned to the cowboys.

"A man leave here sudden you say?"

The two hands faced him. The man they beheld—tall, rugged-looking, who addressed them with a steady eye—seemed to their own seasoned eyes a man to respect. They marked his slinged arm curiously but made a point of not staring.

"They was two," corrected the man in red. "Two rode out."

"Birds of a feather," added his friend. "One skinned on poker debts, the other was just plain mean. I wouldn't trust either of 'em far as I could throw 'em."

"When did they leave?" Clay asked.

The shorter man shrugged, his pale blue eyes squinting. "Must be three, maybe four weeks. . . . Wouldn't you say, Haney?"

"It was midweek, I know that. Me an Curly was headed to town for fence posts. Big Bill catches us at the gate, says them two's gone so he's two men short an' pulls us off to work on the barn roof. Yeah, I recollect it was a Wednesday."

Clay quickly reckoned the days. Wednesday three weeks ago. The barn had burned that Tuesday, the very night before. The barn burned; Danny had lost consciousness; Clay had all but lost his arm; and the next morning two of Lardon's men rode out unexpected.

"These fellas," Clay said grimly, "what are their names, an' what do they look like?"

The men exchanged a look.

"They owe you money, too?" asked the short man.

Clay's eyes narrowed. "I've got other business with 'em."

The cowhand nodded and decided not to pursue it.

"Morgan and Rax. Dirk Morgan an' . . . what was the kid's name?"

"Fred," declared his partner. "Like the yeller dog I had when I's a kid. Ornery little cuss I finally had to shoot. . . . Rax is maybe twenty-five years old. Skinny, yellow-haired—just like that dog. Morgan's about your age, mister. Dark hair an' wears a mustache."

"Dirk Morgan and Fred Rax," Clay repeated, although there was little chance he would forget the names. "Any notion where they headed?"

"Friend, I didn't even know they *was* goin' so I sure can't say where."

"Well," said the man in the vest, "I'd like to help, but they didn't mention a thing."

"Not even just talkin'?" Clay pressed. "No place they'd like to go?"

"Well, 'course Morgan does like his poker. You could try Bodie."

"Bodie?"

The second man nodded. "Haney's right. Morgan's a poker player. He was tight-lipped, but he liked his cards.

"Got into some pretty mean fights over 'em, too. 'Member that cowpoke in the Double Dollar?" he asked Haney. The man shook his head with distaste. "Sheriff wouldn't let him in the Dollar no more after that, said if he couldn't handle his liquor he better keep clear of it. Which is why they may have went to Bodie. Bodie's rough—suit them two fine."

"It's a fair bet," agreed the other man. " 'Bout two days north."

Two days, thought Clay. Already weeks had passed since the pair had left, and another few days would be gone before he arrived himself. Would they still be there, that is, if they'd even gone there at all? Clay had no guarantees, nor was he even sure they'd been involved in the fire. But at least here was a place to start.

Clay studied the men a moment. In their early fifties or so, both were seasoned hands, with hats stained by a thousand miles of trail dust, sweat, campfire smoke, and coffee steam. He noted their clear eyes and open faces. On the frontier a man learned to judge character quickly, and he learned well or died early. Clay felt convinced these two were telling what they knew. Apparently not all Lardon's hands did his bidding so unscrupulously.

"Hey! Wasn't you told to git?"

The harsh voice sounded from the house, and the three men turned.

In the doorway stood Boose. How long he had been there no one knew, but as he stepped out to the porch he wore an ugly expression.

"What was you two jawin' 'bout?" he asked the hands.

Clay said, "Your beef's with me, fella."

Boose turned to him. "Now did you stick around so I could teach you somethin' 'bout takin' orders?"

Clay looked at the man levelly. "Orders from the likes a you mean nothin'. I'll ride in my own good time."

Boose stepped to the edge of the porch. "Anybody ever beat the livin' tar outta you?"

Clay looked at him without flinching. ''Lots have tried.''

''With one hand tied behind their back, I guess, hey?''

''Say, mister,'' said the man in red, uneasily. ''You don't wanna mess with Boose here. . . .''

His friend nodded. ''It's the truth. He's bad medicine.''

Boose stepped off the porch. ''You gimpy saddle tramp,'' he said to Clay. ''I got half a mind to knock that sass outta you, dead arm or not.''

''Careful with that half a mind,'' Clay said coolly. ''You lose it, there'll be wind whistlin' 'tween your ears. . . .''

Boose's face flushed deeply and his eyes narrowed—then he sprang. Clay was ready. He quickly sidestepped, drawing his head back as the other man's fist sailed through empty space where Clay's jaw had been. Turning with the man, twisting his own body, Clay shot out his fist to connect solidly with the other man's jaw; Clay's large, bony knuckles, like marble-size steel ball bearings, connected squarely and snapped the other's head sideways. Boose staggered but remained on his feet; if he had a reputation here as a fighter, Clay could see why. And then Boose was all over Clay, throwing a left and a right, his shoulders behind each swing. The first punch Clay slipped beneath; and the second, aimed at his midsection, he deflected with his forearm. Boose was off balance and Clay crouched and swept his boot in a short crescent behind Boose's heel, catching the other man's ankle and sweeping his weight out from under him. Boose landed hard in the dust.

"My gawd!" exclaimed Haney. "You see that?"

His partner nodded, openmouthed.

But Boose was on his feet again, the look of hatred unmistakable in his eyes.

Clay ducked another haymaker then slipped beneath a left cross, Boose's thick, muscle-knotted arm grazing the top of Clay's back. Clay lashed out sharply, his left fist hooking upward against the man's jaw with a force that by all rights should have ended the fight. Except Boose shook the blow off. Like many big men, Clay realized, Boose counted on brute force—in both doling out and accepting punishment—to win battles.

But Clay knew that brute power alone, although it might win brawls, rarely won real fights; rather, a combination of other skills did, with power perhaps the least important. First came timing, which allowed a man to slip beneath or beyond his opponent's fists, then to dart in with his own in that instant the other man's guard dropped; then came balance, which let one shift one's body weight, and one's direction, in an instant, to put the most behind each blow by putting one's weight behind it; and then came focus, ensuring a fighter's knuckles landed on target rather than glancing off ineffectually or missing altogether. So although Boose threw one haymaker after another, Clay compensated for at least a while. Soon both men were breathing hard, rivulets of sweat streaking their faces and darkly staining their shirts.

Other men had gathered, forming a rough circle

around the fighters. Clay heard snatches of their speech.

"Who is he?"

"Never saw 'im before!"

"What's wrong with his arm? Boose'll kill 'im!"

"No, watch—the man can fight!"

And as Clay slipped again beyond Boose's sledgehammer fists, the more observant watchers realized that by pausing just a moment when exposed, Clay wasn't just finding openings but *making* them, baiting the big man to swing: Boose's big fists swung through empty air, then when Boose was off balance, Clay lashed out and connected solidly.

To these western men it was the best kind of demonstration of skill and courage. Here was a man not only willing to engage an opponent against terrific odds—odds that these men, themselves, might not accept so fast—but who seemed actually to be prevailing against them. To men who faced danger routinely, it showed not just what this man was capable of, but what they might be capable of themselves. It inspired them in the deepest parts of their souls, giving them courage and hope and heart. And so each time Clay's fist connected, the men jerked their heads in short, sharp nods and felt gladdened in their hearts; and each time Boose struck Clay, the men groaned inwardly.

By now both fighters were bloodied: Clay from a cut beneath his eye from the heavy ring Boose wore, and the big ranch hand from a split lip and smashed nose. The two faced each other, breathing heavily. Then an idea seemed to hatch in Boose that was reflected in his small, dull eyes, and he came out of his crouch, coming at Clay again. Boose swung and Clay dodged, and Boose's other fist came up and Clay parried, but then Boose followed with another cross fist—not to Clay's face or midsection, but to his right collarbone; Clay gasped as pain exploded along his side. He fell back, but Boose scurried after him, striking again at the vulnerable spot, and Clay's face went white; instinctively Clay half-turned to protect himself, and the next punishing blow found his kidneys. He staggered.

The men watching grew silent. They had seen this man with but a single fist move like greased lightning and miraculously hold his own against the notorious Boose, but now the sling-armed man was being hit again and again. Boose hammered at the other man's shoulder repeatedly, savagely, and Clay went to one knee.

"My gosh!" one man groaned, and another muttered, "What's holdin' 'im up?"

A ranch hand stepped forward. "He's had enough! *Boose!*" A tall, thin fellow of about forty, the ranch hand squinted. But another man, across the circle, spoke out sharply.

"Butt out, they ain't done yet."

"It ain't a fight no more, Shank. The man's gettin' massacred!"

"I said butt out!"

The man named Rawlins looked across at the gun on Shank's hip and the threat in his eyes. Rawlins scowled. "That's it—I've had it with this outfit. To heck with it and Lardon both.'' Abruptly turning, he stalked off.

Boose, meanwhile, had not let up. Again and again he hit Clay, who somehow refused to fall, though he was past defending himself.

Suddenly a familiar booming voice sounded. ''What's going on? . . . Who's that? . . . *Boose*!''

Brack Lardon came pushing and shoving through the knot of men. Clay raised his head and his locked eyes with the rancher's.

''What—*you*?'' the rancher exclaimed. His eyes grew huge, and all but sputtering with rage he shouted, ''I told you to get out! What do you mean startin' trouble here!'' He turned to his men. ''Get him on his animal an' get him out of here. You men—do it!''

Immediately Shank stepped forward, and lifted Clay roughly from behind. Now two others stepped forward too, although they took Clay's legs more carefully.

''Easy,'' said one, but Shank barked, ''C'mon, hurry up!''

They sat Clay on the Appaloosa, where he slumped forward, blinking and panting, blood staining his shirt. Another man approached with Clay's hat, offering it tentatively. Shank snatched it. Reaching up, he jammed it hard onto Clay's bowed head.

Moving to the front of the horse, Lardon stood beside Clay's bent head. ''You come back here again, you'll get worse—you hear me? Lots worse.''

''I'll be back,'' Clay said softly through swollen lips, his voice harsh. Everyone was quiet.

Lardon shoved his face closer. "What was that? *What'd* you say?"

Swaying in the saddle, blinking as if to focus, Clay turned his bloody face slowly, as if it took great effort, toward the rancher. Blood stained Clay's jaw and blood and dust matted his hair. Although Clay sat hunched and gasping, Lardon saw in his expression a willfulness and determination that the severe beating had not touched.

"I'll be back," Clay repeated hoarsely. "It's not over, Lardon."

The rancher straightened up sharply. "Get him outta here!" he shouted, his face dark. "Shank!" And with that, Shank, who had been holding the Appaloosa's reins, flipped them across the horse's neck and stepped to the animal's hindquarters. Raising his hand high, he shouted, "Git-hey!" and struck the animal hard. Already nervous having sensed its rider slumped across its back, the horse flattened its ears and with eyes wide and nostrils flaring, lunged, nearly spilling Clay off.

"Yeah!" shouted Shank, running after the animal a few steps, and striking it again. "Git, now!"

Lardon stood watching. The rancher's face was still flushed with anger, but beneath it, he could still see the sling-armed man's eyes and could still hear his promise.

Chapter Sixteen

Clay's Appaloosa didn't run far. Out Lardon's gate, another half mile along the trail, and then it slowed to a trot and finally a walk. Confused by its rider's unresponsiveness, it stopped when it reached a small stream. Clay slid from the saddle and landed on his knees. He remained for some time like that, on his knees and the balls of his feet, his head bent, his hand on his thigh, until the Appaloosa moved off. Clay turned and watched the animal step to the edge of the stream and bend its big head to the icy flow. Clay knew he, too, must have water. He staggered to the rounded bedrock, gone orange in the failing light, and lay on his stomach at the water's edge. Pressing his face into the numbing flow, he took long, cooling draughts, feeling relief from the cuts and bruises of Boose's fists. He had been hit before, but rarely taken a worse beating; still, there was satisfaction even now in knowing of the damage he had inflicted in turn. He tugged the bandanna from his pocket and plunged it into the cold, brisk water. The icy flow felt good running past his swollen knuckles and he kept his fist immersed for some time. Then he squeezed out the cold rag and pressed it to the side of his head.

But he knew he must still examine his wound.

Carefully peeling off his sweat-soaked shirt, Clay prodded his injury tenderly. Was there new damage? He didn't know, but all the throbbing and burning of those first days seemed back again. The shoulder area was swollen and discolored, and, touching it gingerly, he sucked air through clenched teeth. But it felt better when he pressed the bandanna to it, and, sitting streamside, he closed his eyes.

Well, he had gotten battered, but not for nothing: The beating had brought information. Dirk Morgan. Fred Rax. The two names were burned into his brain. Had they actually set the fire? He didn't know. Would they be willing to talk? He didn't know that, either. But that he would find them and bring them back—this he *did* know. And if they didn't want to come? Well, he would act on that as he had to.

After the fire all had seemed so hopeless that Clay had lain abed almost not caring if he lived or died. Then Callie's crying had roused him—not just by stirring his sympathy, but by showing how one might endure pain for the sake of others. She had inspired him, and after all the Cookes had done for him Clay knew he would not let them down.

Clay's next move seemed clear. To ride a week or

more to Bodie—and perhaps beyond, depending on where the others' trail took him—he would need extra clothes, his sleeping roll, foodstuffs, and extra cartridges. He pictured his gear, back in the Cookes' pantry.

Clay touched his face, felt the swelling and tenderness beneath his eye that told him it would turn black. His bottom lip was swollen where Boose's ring had cut it. He pictured the Cookes seeing him like this—and immediately decided they must not. It wasn't just that he felt shamed to appear before them so battered (although imagining Callie seeing him this way was somehow especially troubling) it was also that he didn't want to return so obviously needy again. They had done so much already! And not only that, he sensed they would try to stop him. Well, then, he would wait until night, until after they had gone to bed, then ride in quietly to collect his things, and leave. If all went well he would might be back in a few weeks. And if things went badly? Well, so be it. No loss to the Cookes.

It seemed a good plan. As for the hours 'til it was time to ride, he would rest.

He rose still feeling unsteady, but was glad to find he was more clearheaded than before. He immersed his shirt in the stream, feeling it tug in the water's flow, then squeezed it out as best he could and draped it over some bramble bushes. He picketed the horse near a grassy patch, unbuckled its saddle, then dropped the saddle blanket on the ground beneath a hackberry tree, lay down, and, resting his head on the saddle, drew the blanket over him. He tipped his hat over his eyes.

A crescent moon shone in the sky as Clay, opening his eyes, blinked and gauged its position. It was just shy of midnight. Rising stiffly, he carefully flexed and rubbed his shoulder and prodded his ribs. The spot beneath his eye was still tender and swollen.

The night was cool and he was glad to find his shirt mostly dry, if cardboard stiff, and he shivered slightly as he struggled into it. He saddled the horse, mounted up and turned the Appaloosa's head toward the trail.

Clay rode steadily through the hours. When at last the tiny Cooke settlement appeared, he felt a twinge of warm sentiment. He tied his horse at the edge of the wood and made his way quietly toward the house on foot. Grimly he realized that the last time someone had approached the settlement stealthily and under cover of darkness, their intentions had been of arson.

Quietly Clay slipped across the yard. The years had taught him well the importance and technique of silent movement, which often meant the difference between going to sleep hungry or fed, and he took especial care now, thinking Cooke and the others might sleep lighter having learned the price of lack of vigilance. But on the other hand, the tiny family was now exhausted, their grief having sapped their strength.

Nearing the house, Clay felt surprised to see a light at the front window. He moved to the glass and, standing to one side, looked through. On the table sat a lantern, casting its feeble yellow glow around the silent room. Realizing the Cookes had left it burning for him, he felt a pang of tenderness. He moved toward the door. Would it be open? Probably, considering they had left a light for him. When he pressed the latch, it gave beneath his thumb.

Quietly he slipped inside and closed the door. He began to move to the dimly lit pantry, but then stopped, and moved to Callie's door instead.

It was open slightly, a turned-down lantern glow at the edge. Clay eased it open silently, and looked in.

Danny lay on the bed, seemingly peacefully asleep. Callie sat in a rocking chair, her head back, also asleep. Clay watched them a moment, watched them breathing quietly, until, satisfied, he stepped back. Drawing the door closed, he turned to the pantry.

He collected his clothes from hang pegs, stuffed them into his saddlebags lying neatly in a corner and lashed his sleeping roll to them as well. He swung them across his shoulder, moved to the door, and was about to slip out, when, looking back, he thought again. They would notice his things gone and would realize he had been here—stealing in while they slept, taking his things and leaving like a thief in the night with no word of thanks or mention of his plans. He paused, then closed the door, set his things down and moved to the mantelpiece. Finding a pencil stub and some rough sheets of paper, he moved to the table and began to write.

Floyd, Lena and Callie,

I have to leave for a while, but I hope to come back soon. Floyd, please don't sell the spread til I come back. If I am not returned in a couple of weeks, accept my thanks for all you and yours have done.

He began to sign "Clay," but paused, then penciled the word "Will." He set the note in the middle of the table and was about to leave when a door hinge squeaked behind him.

"Will!"

Callie stood in the doorway of the small bedroom wearing a white robe, her braid shining in the yellow light, her eyes wide. She quickly came to him.

"Where have you been?" she whispered urgently, drawing near.

He nodded toward the other door. "Shhh!"

"Will, you're hurt!"

He angled his face away from the light.

"I'm all right. Listen, Callie, how's Danny?"

"The same. He murmurs and moves around some."

"Listen, you got to do something for me. Tell your grandfather not to sell—not 'til I come back. If I'm not back in a few weeks . . . well, then forget me and tell him to go ahead and do what he planned."

She looked up at him. Clay looked down into her eyes and read the emotions there. Leaning forward as her arms came suddenly up to his neck, he kissed her. Then he abruptly turned, and, moving silently to the door, gathered his things and went silently into the night.

Chapter Seventeen

Brack Lardon stood watching his men work the new horse. The animal was a two-year-old they'd found running with a small herd on the south forty, and after flour-breaking it for better than an hour, it was ready to try a man in the saddle rather than the large sack tied across it.

"Okay, Bryan," Lardon shouted, "Climb up an' show 'im who's boss. An' don't be afraid to ride 'im hard!"

The man about to ride moved toward the young animal.

"Go on," Lardon said. "Show 'im!"

Beside Lardon a voice sounded: "You wanted to see me?"

Lardon glanced at Boose, then looked back at the action in the corral.

"Harder!" he shouted. "Force his head up—that's right!" The bucking, kicking horse changed direction sharply, and suddenly the rider pitched off, rolling in the dust.

Lardon scowled. "Where'd you learn to break horses, anyway? Get back on an' stop mollycoddlin' that animal."

Lardon turned to Boose. He squinted at his ranch hand's face, then grinned, shaking his head. "You look terrible."

The other's eyes flashed. Beneath his blackened and half-closed right eye, his face was bruised and swollen, the lower lip twice its normal size. Boose's mouth twisted into a sneer that distorted his face even worse. "I meet 'im again, it's *him* won't look so good."

Lardon nodded mildly as if unimpressed, and turned again to the corral. Slipping a hand into his coat he brought out a cigar, and, from a side pocket, a tiny silver scissors to cut the stogie's tip. He jabbed the cigar into his mouth, lit it, and puffed forcefully, thick blue-gray clouds rising toward the sky.

"Yeah, well I just been wonderin'," the rancher said, his eyes on the horse breaking. "You think that Clay maybe had an extra arm hid somewhere? 'Cause he gave you a *heck* of a fight. That man's a scrapper!"

Boose's face went stone cold. "I ever see that saddle tramp again, Lardon, he'll need buryin'."

The ranch owner shrugged, and studied the cigar's glowing tip. "I'd like to believe that, Boose. 'Specially with him gettin' to be such a burr in my boot.'' He touched the burning end against the rail to round off the ash, then continued watching the horse breaking.

''Now here's what you do. Saddle up an' take a ride. Those two loose mouths Haney and Johnson said Morgan and Rax might be headed to Bodie, so I expect that's where Clay's headed, too. Fine. You know the country. Take a shortcut or two Clay don't know, ride hard, an' you should be able to cut 'im off somewhere. You can manage that, can't you? Catch up with a cripple fella?''

The other man glared.

''An' then you finish things,'' Lardon continued. ''Understand? So he don't nose into my business no more.''

Boose's eyes narrowed and a slow smile spread his cracked lips.

''All right,'' said the rancher. ''That's all. Now get goin', you don't got time to waste. . . . Oh, and listen, don't get in no more fistfights with the man. You get hurt out there by yourself, there won't be nobody to help you.''

The hired man's lips pressed tightly and his eyes flashed. Lardon didn't bother to look around but only waved his hand for Boose to go. The ranch hand left.

Lardon smiled to himself. *Yeah,* he thought. *Keep 'im mean. Probably help get the job done.*

Chapter Eighteen

The morning sun found Clay in a small camp several miles north of the Cooke homestead. When the moon was bright, as it had been last night, and the countryside not especially treacherous, he didn't mind night riding. His shoulder ached and another day's rest would doubtless have helped, but he wanted to start out as soon as he could. The fresher the two men's trail, the easier it would be to follow.

As the sun's rays slanted down across the hills, Clay checked the Appaloosa, then set to building a fire. Having had none last night—it had been all he could do to picket the horse before turning in—he felt desperate for hot coffee. He broke a handful of twigs, set them atop birch-bark peelings from his saddlebags, positioned some thicker sticks in a crosshatch above them, and lit the oily birch with a match.

From his canteen he filled the dented coffeepot, which he hung by its thin metal handle on a notched stick he drove into the dirt. As the pot swung above the flames, he settled back to examine his collarbone and shoulder.

Despite yesterday's pain and swelling, even these few hours' rest had made a difference. Whether it was his good health generally or his determination to push on, he felt strong enough to continue.

Still, yesterday's battle had taught him a critical lesson: To go against another man toe-to-toe, pitting his single fist against an opponent's two, would be foolhardy. And if Morgan and Rax were cut from the same cloth as Boose, this might prove especially dangerous. Clay had recognized in Boose a viciousness that was nearly out of control. When Clay caught up with Lardon's other two henchmen he would be questioning them, likely accusing them, and intending to bring them back to a place they would not want to go. He would need resources other than his fist.

Standing, he poured steaming coffee into a battered metal cup, swallowed several scalding gulps of the bitter brew, then moved to his saddlebags. He undid the buckle and brought out his gunbelt, the gun in its holster. Reaching in again he removed a compact, tightly wrapped object in oilcloth which, after he'd settled down onto his knees, he unrolled on the ground. There lay a second Colt, the other's companion, in a matching left-hand holster; the gun glistened beneath an oil-film Clay had applied against the harshness of the coming winter. He slipped the

.44 from its leather, wiped the weapon clean with a rag, and hefted it. It felt somewhat awkward, but not altogether so, and this Clay attributed to his having worked over the years at keeping practiced with both hands. An old Texas Ranger had advised him once "be able to ride long, bluff when you need to, and draw fast and shoot straight with either hand," and Clay had taken the advice to heart. Now he cracked open the barrel, spun the cylinder, and cocked and released the pistol several times, squeezing the trigger but easing the hammer down with his thumb so as not to dry-snap the weapon. Although some years had passed since he had regularly fired left-handed, it was a skill that, once learned well, a man did not forget.

Setting the gun aside, he turned to its holster. Like other men who liked a rig that was versatile, Clay had had a saddlemaker stitch to the gunbelt four small, finely crafted brass buckles that secured each holster to the gunbelt separately. Attaching the left-draw holster now only took moments. He stood, but now suddenly realized that strapping the gunbelt around his waist might prove far more complicated. After deliberating a moment he jammed the buckle end into the front of his jeans, wound the tongue end around his back as far as he could reach, then stuffed it into his right side. Reaching around front again, he grasped the tongue, pulled it across his hips and attempted to fit the ends together—promptly dropping the whole rig. He swore under his breath and tried again. And again. The fourth or fifth time, however, he managed to feed the tongue through the buckle, and when he nudged the metal prong into place, securing the belt, he nearly whooped with relief. How frustrating to have to devise new ways of doing things he took for granted! But he must play the cards he was dealt and could only hope things would get easier.

He was ready now to practice drawing and firing. He drove a half-dozen foot-length sticks into the ground, stepped back twenty paces, glanced at the Appaloosa to be sure he was tied (not that the animal was especially gun-shy) and then, looking again toward his targets, he set his feet wide and breathed calmly. A cricket chirped somewhere, and Clay chose its next chirp as his signal. He waited. Listened. Felt utterly relaxed, yet utterly ready. *Tweet.* . . . His hand blurred and the gun roared, the Colt bucking as fragments of rock chipped and sprang away perhaps two feet wide of the first stick. Clay set his mouth and returned the sidearm to its holster. He eyed the stick, waited, and drew again—this time not firing but only bringing the pistol to where he would fire. Then he reholstered and repeated the move several times.

There were secrets to the fast draw and "practicing parts" was one: You reduced the draw to its component moves, its parts, and practiced each, training each muscle or muscle group to do its job, the shoulder and arm bringing the hand to the grip, the fingers curling around the wood, the index finger finding the trigger, and so on. Only once each was good, *very* good, did you combine them into a single seamless motion. A dozen different motions were involved in the draw, and what you did was get them all to do their job well and not wait for each other but sort of trust each would be there, ready, when its time came.

Clay had first learned of practicing parts when no more than Danny's age when a stranger who wore twin guns stayed briefly at the fort. His aunt and uncle owned a small store, and Clay had hung around afternoons. At the time, young Clay did not know the man's profession, just as he did not understand much of what the man had told him—about practicing parts, as the man had called it, and "moving round" and other things the man spoke of; only years later did it all begin to make sense. Now, of course, Clay knew the man's occupation well enough, just as he understood why his uncle and aunt had wanted him to keep clear of him. Clay had never learned the gunfighter's name.

Clay remembered "moving round": "There's no straight lines in nature," the man had said, "an' there's a lesson there about the quick draw, too." You lost time moving at angles, moved quicker in arcs. In the quick draw, it meant you saved time if you changed the motion of your arm from jerky right-angle movements that called for you to redirect your motion several times (first one direction, then another, at some sharp new angle), to moving "round" instead.

Clay practiced. His hand moved to the pistol, snatched it, lifted it and continued upward, but then described a smooth, circular motion and brought it with the barrel bearing on his target. He faced the stick and cleared his mind. Again he listened. *Tweet!*

He drew, and the Colt's rapid-fire thunder sent the sticks leaping and jerking to a deafening symphony. Draw and fire, draw and fire . . .

When finally he was hitting the sticks consistently, snapping them off clean lower and lower until nothing remained of them aboveground at all, he thought, *so much for the first part.* But he still could not reload quickly, and in going against two men this would be a deadly liability.

He needed a second gun.

Clay looked down at the holster on his other, right hip. Reaching across, he drew the pistol from it backward, flipped the gun around in his hand, readying it for action. But the move had been awkward and uncomfortable, and far too time-consuming. He studied the belt for some moments before knowing what he must do.

In his saddlebags he found a length of rawhide cord; drawing from its sheath at the back of his saddle his bone-handled bowie knife, its wide blade flashing brightly in the sun, he unbuckled the gunbelt—regretfully, thinking of what it had taken to put it on—and sat with the knife and cord. He unbuckled the right holster and cut into the belt part, working at the sturdy leather, making a series of quarter-inch slices, then threading the rawhide through, and through the top of the holster. It took a while and looked rough, but when he was done, he thought it should serve him.

This time it took only three tries to put on the belt.

He slipped the pistol into the now backward-mounted holster and, reaching across, grasped the grip and slid the gun several times.

For the next half hour he practiced, drawing first on one side, then the other. There was no question the cross-draw felt unnatural at first, but after a half hour it felt better, and a half hour later more comfortable yet. By the end of the morning, although by no means altogether expert, Clay had reason to feel some confidence about his new skill.

Chapter Nineteen

Boose lay on his belly forty feet above the river, positioned among rocks overlooking where the trail ended at the coursing water. The sun sat low, glinting on the fast-moving flow, and Boose felt satisfied with the spot he had chosen. Not only was it remote, it also suited Boose's purpose because of the time of day. Clay would stop here for the night. To cross, a rider must wade his horse through chest-deep water, and with the late-afternoon coolness, Clay would wait until morning: To cross tonight would mean continuing on the other side in wet clothes, but even more importantly, it meant Clay's horse would be wet. Though a determined rider might willingly suffer discomfort himself, to risk the health of his animal would be foolhardy. Yes, Clay would camp here. It was this scheming that had driven Boose to ride hard all day and, taking shortcuts no stranger would know, to reach this place well before the sling-armed man. Boose's tied horse was out of earshot over the hill, and although the animal was badly exhausted, Boose didn't care. He looked forward to riding Clay's Appaloosa.

Squinting down at the trail, his Winchester in the crook of his elbow, Boose again congratulated himself on his vantage point. He would see anyone approaching a hundred yards uptrail, and could see also where a rider would rein in along the bank to gauge the river's flow and depth and choose his landing point on the far bank.

The rifleman levered a cartridge into the Winchester's chamber; now was the time when he needn't worry about the sound. Some men could hear the telltale click long before it seemed possible, and to Boose, Clay seemed this type.

Boose would take his time.

Again he peered down, drawing a bead where the horseman would appear. At this range Boose could easily squeeze a round into his target dead center, punching him out of his saddle before he even heard the shot. Boose lowered the rifle and fingered his broken nose. It was hurting again. His prodding made him suddenly sneeze, which only hurt more. He cursed under his breath. He turned to spit, but the motion caused him only more pain, as a piercing twinge stabbed across the back of his neck where his head had rocked from Clay's punishing knuckles. Boose curled his lip. Well, the sling-armed man would pay. For Boose's pain, yes, but also for making him look like a fool in front of the others.

Scowling across the landscape, Boose settled in to wait.

The trail's downward slope and its thickening vegetation signaled a stream or small river ahead; Clay read the land as any who knew it could.

He had been riding long. This was country where backtrails likely ran, and following the right ones Clay likely would make better time. But he was unfamiliar with them and knew it was better to lose a little time staying on the main trail than lose much—and exhaust his animal—by having to backtrack because he'd come to some dead end. He shifted in his creaking saddle, reined in, and lifted his canteen, hanging by its cord over the horn. Biting out the cork, he shifted it to the corner of his mouth and poured the tepid water down his throat. His side was acting up again—not badly, but enough to make the pain a presence, and he felt half-inclined to stop for the night right here. True, he might make a few miles more tonight, but not many, and he would welcome the rest. Squinting ahead, he saw that just about anyplace off-trail would do. But then he thought again about the men he pursued, who had reason to put as much ground behind them as possible. Men like these you followed close and hard. Grimly Clay recorked the canteen, flicked the reins and set the Appaloosa again in motion.

Soon he heard the rush of coursing water. It was a fair-size current, perhaps a hundred yards ahead to judge by the sound. The horse had been smelling it for some time, moving more urgently, excitedly, its head high, ears perked, wanting the cold, fresh flow. Clay rode to the water's edge. He could see where the trail continued on the far bank, but with the growing coolness he reined in to weigh his options.

"Hold it!" The voice came from Clay's left, and above him. He froze, reacting instinctively to its nearness and tone of menace. If the other man had wanted to just shoot Clay, he had had ample chance already. And if he had no gun, there would be no harm in waiting. Clay said nothing, only squinted grimly up toward the rocks. A raucous laugh erupted. From behind cover slowly stood John Boose. Clay noted the Winchester in his grip, leveled, no mistake about it, at Clay's heart. Clay regarded him with steely eyes.

"That's good," Boose continued. "You know when to freeze. I got the trigger half-squeezed, an' if you'd a moved sudden, you'd be done." He smiled. "I guess you remember me."

Clay sat his horse. "I remember."

"I was gonna take you right in the saddle," Boose said, "but then I thought, hey, you'd never know it was me."

The man stood fifty feet away. Clay thought of nudging the Appaloosa's ribs to half-turn the animal so he could try jumping clear, but the ruse would be obvious. As if reading his thoughts, Boose said, "You hold that animal steady. You even think a makin' a break, you're dead before he takes a step."

Clay steadied his mount. "What do you want, Boose," he asked flatly.

"Now don't get impatient on me. An' don't dismount just yet," the rifleman said. "I don't want you runnin' anywheres on me." Boose suddenly smiled. "Now what you got there—a left-draw holster, is it?" He leveled the Winchester more firmly. "Slick! Tell you what, why don't you just grab the hammer there with two fingers"—he braced his aim of the rifle—"an' ease 'er from the leather real slow, an' drop 'er to the ground. Then we'll finish what we started yesterday."

Clay followed Boose's orders. "This your idea or Lardon's?"

"Lardon's got his reasons, but this suits me fine . . ."

As Clay's pistol clattered to the ground, Boose grinned. "Now I feel better." And suddenly Clay realized Boose had not seen, and could not see, the pistol riding Clay's right hip. It was hidden by the horse's neck and perhaps the waning light, and anyway Boose had no reason to expect Clay to be wearing a second revolver, let alone on his injured side. Clay held his horse steady.

Boose began to move forward, the rifle barrel wavering as he picked his way down the slope. It was precisely as he raised his foot to step over a branch that Clay squeezed his horse's belly with his boot heel and leaned ever so slightly left, half-turning the animal.

"That's fine," Clay said. "Right there's about perfect, *pard*." He reached across to rest his hand on the revolver's wood grip.

The rifleman stopped in midstride. He was on inclined ground, the rifle in his hands, but its barrel aimed downward. Boose's self-assured grin dissolved as a look of surprise flashed on his face, and deep color crept up his neck.

Clay looked at him levelly.

"You can put it down an' live, or you can try to raise it, an' I'll kill you. I don't want to—there's no reason you should die here. It's up to you," he said.

Neither man moved. Clay watched the other's eyes. And then Clay saw it: A tiny tightening of Boose's mouth that telegraphed his intent. Clay was moving then, his hand a blur. In an instant his fingers curled around the smooth, wood grip, his arm doing its own work pulling the heavy Colt clear of leather, drawing it across his body in a motion as fluid and natural as a man pointing his finger. The rifle pivoted upward, but the Colt exploded and its heavy, lead charge knocked Boose back a step, as if from a blow, his face registering surprise: The Winchester boomed, and something plucked sharply at Clay's shirt. Boose's hand was working by reflex, levering another shell into the chamber, and Clay had to fire again and this slug caught Boose in his left shoulder and spun him, and the Winchester clattered against stone.

The whole thing lasted perhaps three seconds.

Clay sat ahorse looking at the fallen man for some moments. Then Clay dismounted.

Chapter Twenty

Clay spent the next day riding. He had buried Lardon's gunman off-trail on the side of the hill the evening before, digging a shallow grave with his bowie knife, then placed a number of large stones atop the mound. The chore had proved time-consuming and laborious, but as work that must be done, Clay had done it.

Any questions or doubts he might still have had about Lardon's involvement, Clay laid to rest with the dead man. Why else would Lardon send Boose after Clay? The rancher's desperate directive could only mean Clay was on track.

He rode with Boose's horse tied behind him and the dead man's gunbelt in his saddlebags. Clay had forded the river early that morning and with the sun now high, his trouser legs and his mount's belly were nearly dry. If he continued at this pace he would reach Bodie by next day.

Bodie, Montana, lay dug in deep among the Wyatt Hills, a small town its founders had settled four years ago under the mistaken belief the nearby hills contained gold. Two businessmen-brothers from Boston, John and Mike Gullifti—speculators with visions of extending their fortune—hearing a rumor of a fat vein discovered recently, had journeyed west to snatch their share of what they hoped would prove a jackpot. But they didn't come as prospectors. Realizing they knew nothing of the work (which, anyway, seemed too dangerous) they had a different plan. For as they saw it, they could either prospect for gold themselves and gamble on a long list of uncertainties, which ranged from being robbed and murdered by claim jumpers, bitten by rattlesnakes, killed in some accident out in rough country, or simply finding no gold, or they could open a saloon where those who had already found gold and managed to hold onto it would come spend it. And since the Gullifti brothers also figured that those presumably toughest, shrewdest, and most tenacious of gold hunters might also prove the ones who needed most to blow off steam, they reasoned that anyone who sold them whiskey, cards, and women might rake in profits hand over fist. So they traveled west to build the granddaddy of all saloons, to attract those from miles around who had found gold and sought someplace to spend it.

But after building the saloon—an undeniably impressive-looking building, with a half-dozen windows across its broad, two-story front, space at the hitch-rails for a good thirty horses, and tall, gold lettering that read GULLIFTI'S SALOON up top—they saw no gold come to Bodie. The one find had been all. The gold never did pan out, but the luxurious saloon still stood. Riders occasionally stopped in, curious, but not nearly so many as the brothers had hoped for, and anyway, these customers weren't wealthy prospectors who came in with bulging leather pouches heavy with gold dust and nuggets, but drifters and saddle tramps of a distinctly poorer sort. The saloon was founded on a misconception, had been built with money some said was ill-gotten back East anyway, so maybe it was only fair it was destined to fail. The brothers sold out cheap soon after. The new owner didn't even try to keep it up so that the building's former grandeur, now that it was going to seed, made it seem doubly run-down and mean, which went for the people it attracted, too. The saloon spawned Bodie's reputation for rough gambling and rough men and was a place people went for hard times.

Clay rode into Bodie just after noon. The sun hung high casting sharp shadows. As Clay rode slowly up Main Street, his reins loosely in hand, he led Boose's animal, still tied loosely to the Appaloosa's tail.

Seeing the saloon from a distance, Clay felt surprised and impressed. Only as he rode closer did he notice that the gold gilt letters were worn and flaking, the water in the troughs was brackish and brown, and the windows were webbed with bullet holes. The saloon's builders obviously had anticipated better times than had materialized. Clay looked up the street at other buildings: Matt Novak's hardware, Holt's general store, and the Parker Hotel. At the end of the short, dirt-packed street he spotted a sign that read: ZINNY'S LIVERY. Touching his heels to the Appaloosa's ribs, he rode toward it.

Zinny's was a ramshackle building with finger-wide spaces between its cracked, sun-bleached boards, and double doors that sagged on their hinges.

Out front, Clay swung down from the saddle and squinted into the building's gloomy interior. The smells of horse sweat and hay filled the air, and feeling hungry and thirsty, he was thinking about food. "Hello," he called.

"Yeah, yeah—I'm comin'," came a voice from within. The thump of boots on earth sounded and a tall, rangy, quick-eyed man appeared, with stringy, dark yellow hair falling over his eyes. He looked about twenty-five years old. He swiped the hair away and cast a curious eye at Clay's pinned sleeve, but then, seeming to take the measure of the man, he darted his eyes away.

"Help you, mister?" he muttered sullenly.

"The Appaloosa needs to be brushed and fed," Clay said. "The other horse I mean to sell."

The sullen fellow glanced quickly at the second animal with furtive, appraising eyes.

"We-l-l-l," he said, suddenly with a drawl, "don't know as I need any more just now. . . . I sure can't pay much. . . ."

"A livery can always use a sound animal for the right price," Clay said. "Listen, it's not money I want. Take care a the Appaloosa and give me some information, an' we'll call it square.''

The other man immediately perked up, but the next instant his eyes grew wily. ''You know, mister, a stranger rides in givin' away a horse, saddle an' gear. . . . To some that might look funny. Know what I mean? They'd wonder where he got 'em.''

Impatiently, Clay said, ''The man that owned 'im is dead—that horse'll do him no good now. Now don't waste my time, I got things to tend to. What I want to know is, did two fellas ride in 'bout two weeks ago, put their horses up?''

''Well, 'course a lotta men come through. . . .''

''One's young, the other's my age. The young one's blond-haired, the other's dark with a mustache.''

The livery owner rubbed his chin. ''We-el-l-l, come to think of it, two fellas *did* ride in like you say. . . . Still in town, in fact. Their animals are right there.'' The man pointed, and Clay stepped close to the roan and cutback the other had indicated, which were standing in adjacent stalls. On their flanks he saw a familiar brand: Big B over L. The same as over Brack Lardon's gate.

Clay's eyes darted to the two saddles resting across the stall rails. He flipped aside the first bag's cover flap and peered inside.

''Say, now, mister,'' the livery man interrupted.

Clay ignored him and brought out a stirrup. Tilting it to the light, he studied its familiar oversized, twelve-pointed rowel and distinctive Mexican-style design. Setting it on the rail Clay fished from his shirt pocket the wheel he'd been carrying. The two were identical, a matched pair. Clay glanced at the livery man, who had been watching, then dug into the saddlebag again. This time he brought out a spur whose rowel was missing altogether, its back-mounting bent, the tiny axle pin gone. Clay turned to the livery man.

"These two men—where would I most likely find 'em?"

Max Zinny licked his lips then said in a confidential voice. "Want to see 'em pretty bad, huh?"

Clay's eyes narrowed.

" 'Cause I think I can help," the thin man said, "but maybe my trouble's worth somethin'?" He smiled and winked conspiratorially.

Clay moved fast. Suddenly his fist was jammed beneath the other man's jaw, twisting his shirt collar tight against his throat.

"Mister, I've had my fill a you. You'll answer what I asked *now!*"

The other man, pressed back against the wood plank, raised his open hands. "Okay, okay!" Clay loosened his grip. "I seen 'em just a while ago, a hour ago . . . at Gullifti's!"

Clay released the liveryman, collected the spurs and rowel, and put them into his own saddlebags. "Now you tend my animal good," he said. "An' if you happen to see those two before I do, don't mention I was askin' after 'em." With that Clay was out the door.

The livery man waited a moment then moved to

the doorway, watching Clay cut diagonally across the street toward Gullifti's. Then Zinny slipped out and, rubbing his neck and glancing over his shoulder, walked hurriedly in the opposite direction.

Chapter Twenty-one

Zinny thought about going to the sheriff about the stranger who'd come in, giving away a horse and gear for nothing, but Rich McDonald was out of town and anyway, the livery man knew there wasn't a chance he was about to involve the law when it meant he might lose everything if it turned out to be stolen property. Of course Zinny could also do as the stranger ordered: Nothing. But Zinny wasn't going to just sit back, either—not when there was a chance of earning a quick dollar.

At the Parker Hotel he glanced again over his shoulder, then cut sharply in through the door.

The small lobby, with its dingy, threadbare red carpet, wilted geraniums hanging in window pots and worn, overstuffed armchairs was empty except for a man behind the counter. Sitting on a tall stool, the white-haired old man wore glasses perched half down his nose. He had a vest that may have fit once, but now hung as loose and roomy as a horse blanket. His wrinkled shirt was rolled to his elbows, showing parchment-pale skin. He was bent over a newspaper but he looked up as Zinny came clomping in, and promptly scowled with distaste.

"Zinny," he said.

"I'm in a hurry, Parker," said the livery man, "so don't start jawin' with me. Listen, those two fellas rode in the other week, the young light-haired one and the older mustached fella. They in their rooms?"

Parker frowned. "Heck, I don't watch ever'body comes in an' goes out all day long."

"Well which are their rooms—hurry up, Parker, this is business!"

The older man squinted at the register. "Morgan and Rax—three and four, across from each another." He looked up to find the livery man moving toward the stairs. "But they don't seem the type to like company unexpected."

"You let *me* worry 'bout that," Zinny called, reaching for the bannister.

At the top of the stairs, along a dim hallway lit by a single grimy skylight, Zinny quickly found doors three and four. Actually, the number 3 seemed to have fallen off some time ago, its outline barely readable. Zinny stepped close, listened a moment, looked behind him at room four, then turned back to three and tentatively knocked. Immediately bedsprings sounded. Then nothing. Zinny waited. Still nothing. He cleared his throat and raised his hand to knock again, but before his knuckles could touch wood the lock snapped and the door sprang open—and from it thrust a pistol barrel, aimed squarely at Zinny's face. With wide eyes the livery man saw the thumbed-back hammer, and a grizzled face behind the weapon.

"What you want?" snarled Dirk Morgan. Unshaved and shirtless, the big-chested man stood barefoot in half-buttoned jeans, his reddened eyes staring.

The livery man forced a weak smile and showed his palms for the second time in an hour.

"Easy, mister, it's just me. . . . Max Zinny? Remember, you left your horses with me?"

Morgan didn't lower the Colt. Instead he eyed the other man closely, then bent forward to peer up and down the hallway. "Somethin' wrong with 'em?" he demanded, focusing again on Zinny.

"No, no, nothin' like that! I just . . . well, I got some information for you."

Morgan waited.

"See, there's a fella lookin' for you," Zinny added. "He rode in just a while ago and asked after you an' your partner. I thought you'd wanna know!"

Morgan stepped into the hallway, pulling the door closed, and moved barefoot across the faded carpet. Keeping an eye on the livery man, he rapped sharply with the butt of his Colt on the door opposite. "Rax!"

Floorboards creaked. "Morgan?"

"Open up!"

The door swung open. Rax stood with his unbuttoned shirt hanging outside his trousers. He also held a pistol.

"Whozzat, the livery guy?" he said.

Morgan pushed Zinny past his partner, followed him in, and closed the door. He turned to the livery man, who stood nervously beside the bed. "Start talkin' " the mustached man ordered.

Zinny cleared his throat and, looking from one man to the other, smiled weakly. He was beginning to think he had gotten in over his head.

"Well, ah, this fella," he began, "he come askin' for you—described you both. . . ."

"What'd you say?" Morgan demanded.

"Oh . . . well, nothin'. I kept my mouth shut!" Zinny rubbed his knuckles nervously. "But he, ah, spotted your horses. He seemed to recognize the brand."

"What else?" Morgan said, keeping his eyes on the livery man.

"Well, he started pokin' through your saddlebags. I told 'im it was private property, but he paid no mind. Found a pair a spurs, one with a wheel broke off. Then he pulled another spur from his pocket with a wheel just like it—"

"Where'd he find that!" Rax blurted.

Morgan squinted at the livery man. "This fella—what's he look like?"

"Oh, he's easy to spot. Big an' rough-lookin', but the thing about 'im is, he's got but one good arm—the other's all slinged-up."

"One good *arm*?" blurted Rax.

"But he's still no one to mess with," Zinny warned. "Take it from me. . . ."

"An' he's alone?" Morgan asked. "Nobody with 'im at all?"

"Not that I saw," the livery man said.

"What you think?" Rax asked his partner. "Just one fella by himself?"

"Could be others out of sight or close behind," Morgan said. "Listen, if they put a reward on us, there'll be a whole passel a fellas gunnin' for us." Morgan spat on the floor then looked sharply at the livery man. "All right, weasel, you told us—now get out!"

"Sure—sure!" Zinny said, ducking his head even as he moved toward the door. But then, as if unable to stop himself, he added, "Ahh, I just thought you boys would wanna know—that you'd be *grateful*, if you know what I mean. . . ."

"We're grateful," Morgan snarled. "So grateful we're not gonna kick your sorry butt down those stairs."

The livery man turned and quickly reached for the door. But Morgan stepped forward and shoved a hand against it. "Keep in mind if you figger to play both ends against the middle an' tell him you seen us, it'll be the last bargainin' you do, pardner."

Zinny nodded vigorously. "Yessir! Don't you worry, mum's the word!" Morgan removed his hand and the next moment the other man was gone.

"So what you think?" Rax asked.

"I don't know who he is, but I know what it's about. An' if there's a reward, there'll be more behind. Gawd, though, a man with just one good arm. . . . That low-down dog Lardon must've tipped 'im off."

"Lardon? But he'd be hangin' himself too."

"Maybe they pinned something on him an' he got scared—figured to give us up an' save his own hide. With his money they won't touch him. That's rich man's justice. Listen, all's I know is *somebody's* trackin' us, and where there's one there'll be more."

Rax pulled on his boots. "You think he's a bounty hunter?"

"With a bad arm?" said Morgan. "I never heard a any such thing—nor of any marshal, neither." He spat again. "I don't know who he is, but one thing's sure: Nothin' good'll come of him findin' us. Not with the trouble we left behind. That wasn't just some barn burnin', we're talkin' murder." He frowned. "Hurry an' get dressed."

Rax tucked in his shirt. "Yeah, well, it wasn't me said let's leave the kid. . . ."

Standing at the window, squinting down at the street, Morgan turned sharply. "What was that?"

"I'm just sayin' maybe if we'd drug 'im out—"

"Then he'd a described us to everybody and we wouldn't a got *this* far. Get this straight, Rax: To a jury, you'll be as guilty as I am. We both left 'im in that barn. If the law catches us, we both swing." He moved to the bedpost, grabbed Rax's gunbelt and tossed it to the younger man. "C'mon, we gotta get outta here. We'll head to Missoula where we'll have some room to get lost in. Now, I'll go pull on clothes an' get my gear, but meanwhile you go by the livery, get the horses."

"What, me go down by myself?"

"Rax, there's no time to lose. I'll be right behind you!"

Rax scowled but then moved to the door; passing the bureau he snagged the bottle off it and upended it over his mouth. He cursed, and flung the empty bottle into the corner where it smashed.

"Too early for that, anyway," Morgan said.

"It's never too early for that," said Rax. "I'll pick up another on my way out."

"Rax, didn't you hear me? I said we gotta *go*! Forget the liquor—there's time for that later. Just get the horses!"

When Rax had left, Morgan hurried to his own room. The bed was rumpled, its blanket and his clothes strewn across the floor. He gathered them up, stepped to the window, and dressed watching the street.

Of course he hadn't told Rax the main reason for sending him out ahead: If anyone were out there watching, or if the livery man were part of a trap, Morgan wanted to find out beforehand.

Strapping on his gun, Morgan watched Rax leave the front of the building and head up the street.

Fred Rax's throat felt dry. Striding toward the livery, he squinted ahead at the saloon across the street. Soon he and Morgan would be running again, riding clear of towns. Who knew the next chance he'd get to buy a bottle? And who said Morgan ran this show, anyway? Glancing back at the hotel, Rax suddenly cut diagonally across the street. Forget Morgan. This would only take a second.

Morgan, watching from the window, scowled.

Chapter Twenty-two

"That's right, the young one had light hair, an the other wore a mustache. . . . But they ain't been in here all morning."

With a bar towel in hand, Bob Gale stood where he had paused in polishing glasses to face Clay across the shining bartop. "These two fellas," Gale continued warily, "they friends a yours?" The bartender had of course noticed Clay's slinged arm, but the big, serious-looking stranger still had a look about him—in the stern eyes, and hard cast to the mouth—that said he was no one to cross.

"*Friends,*" Clay growled. "No, not friends. . . . They pulled some bad business near Sharpton an' I'm here to take 'em back."

Dusty columns of sunlight slanted through the saloon's windows, showing shiny patches of floorboard where spilled beer had dried.

"Bad business, huh?" repeated the barkeep, noticeably relaxing when he heard Clay and the others weren't cohorts. "Well, I ain't surprised. I been tendin' bar long enough to know trouble when I see it, an' those two are it."

A short, powerfully built man, the bartender had a thick neck, beefy forearms, and waxed handlebar mustache. "The other night the younger one poured back a few an' started mouthin' off. Cost me business, I know that. Folks leave early when a stranger's lookin' for trouble. I got myself a little persuader under the bar"—he reached underneath and drew out a blue-steeled sawed-off .12-gauge shotgun,—"but I save 'er only for real trouble. Haul 'er out too frequent an' she loses 'er authority." The bartender returned the weapon to its place. "That boy's partner was just as bad. Got in a game a five-card stud an' dang if he didn't nearly draw on a fella! But the other backed down when he seen this one's eyes." The barkeep shook his head. "Sheriff McDonald's outta town 'til tomorrow, don't it figure? . . . But yet, they're a pair, those two—like you said, bad business." The man swiped at the bartop's already gleaming surface.

"Well, I appreciate the help," Clay said.

Boots sounded on the boardwalk then, and Clay turned as the bat-wing doors burst open. In strode a tall, young blond-haired man wearing a sour expression. ''Gimme a bottle a rotgut!'' he ordered. ''An' fast! I'm on my way outta this stinkin' one-horse—''

The words caught in his throat and his step faltered as his eyes fixed on the man at the bar—a man with a sling-arm and eyes focused intently upon him. Before the startled blond man could act, though, the other man's hand moved and a Colt appeared, aimed directly at the younger man's heart.

''Not another step,'' Clay said. ''An' you even think a movin' for your iron an' you're dead before you hit the floor. By your look I'd say you know what I'm after.''

''Say, now, mister,'' said the younger man, ''I never ever seen you in m'life, you got no quarrel with me!'' He turned to the staring bartender. ''I never even *seen* this fella!'' he said, and then, turning again to Clay, his voice adopted the volume and indignation of someone accused unfairly. ''You got no call pullin' guns on strangers! I come in for a bottle, mindin' my own business—''

''Stow it!'' Clay ordered. ''Just unbuckle your gunbelt and set it on the bar.''

The younger man frowned. ''The heck I will! You'll have to shoot me first!''

Clay eyed him coolly. ''That's your choice, Rax.''

The younger man looked startled. But then his eyes got cagey and his thin lips stretched into the semblance of a smile. ''What'd you call me—Rax? Why, heck, stranger, you got the wrong man!'' He half-turned to the bartender. ''My name's Hanson! Pete Hanson!''

Clay's Colt remained leveled. He thumbed back the hammer. "The gunbelt. I won't ask again."

Rax's eyes flashed hatred as his mouth drew into two thin white lines. His palms rose to shoulder height. "Okay, easy now! I don't know who you are, stranger, but a man points a pistol at me, I listen. . . ." Slowly his hands moved to his belt buckle. "See? Jus' like you say. . . ."

Morgan stood across the street, scowling. What was keeping Rax? He'd gone into the saloon despite Morgan's orders, but even Rax wouldn't be so dumb as to drink there, would he? Keeping in the shade of the hotel porch, Morgan glanced up and down the street. No sign of a sling-armed man anywhere, but that didn't mean he wasn't here. Unless . . . had that idiot liveryman made the whole thing up? Figured to touch them for a few dollars? If so, Morgan would settle with him on the way out. Raising a calloused hand to his hat, he pulled the brim low and stepped onto the sun-bright street. A buckboard rumbled past, a boy led a mule on a rope, and others went about their business as Morgan cut diagonally across toward the saloon.

"An' don't forget that rawhide cord around your neck," Clay ordered.

Rax had emptied his pockets, setting their contents on the bartop. The makings of cigarettes, a box of matches, some loose coins, and a couple of .45 slugs lay in a heap.

"But that's my money!" he objected.

"Put it with the rest," Clay said, gesturing with the pistol.

Rax did so. "Barkeep," he said, "you're a witness here. This fella's stealin' m'money!"

"No one's stealing anything from you," Clay said. "Barkeep, you count it, if you don't mind."

The bartender loosened the strings and turned the leather pouch upside down close to the counter; several thick gold coins clattered onto the bar.

Gale raised his eyebrows. "Some caboodle!" he said. After a moment's counting he announced, "Sixty-five dollars. A healthy travelin' kit!"

"What'd you do to get all this, Rax?" Clay asked.

"Me? I had me some business dealings. Not that it's your concern. . . ."

Clay eyed him hard. "I just bet you did. All right, where's your partner?"

Standing at the edge of one of the saloon's front windows, Dirk Morgan squinted against the pane's reflection. What he saw made him freeze: Rax, standing at the bar, face-to-face with a man pointing a gun at his belly. Morgan looked harder. Sure enough, the stranger's right arm hung in a sling. Who *was* he?

Morgan glanced up the street toward the livery. He could get his horse, ride out, and be done with Rax once and for all. It was the younger man's own fault he'd gotten caught, and if Morgan left now, he might even win a head start. True, Rax might prove useful if things came down to a shoot-out against their pursuers later. But Morgan would attract less attention traveling alone.

Morgan's mind raced with possibilities.

Of course, now that Rax was caught, the young idiot would confess everything: that it had been Morgan who struck down the boy and Morgan who had insisted they leave him. Rax would spill everything, hoping to save his own skin. Then not just the sling-armed man, but others, too, would be after Morgan, and harder than ever.

Morgan quickly looked around. In both the saloon and the street, at least for now, the sling-armed man was alone. And his back was to the door.

Dropping his hand to his gunbelt, taking care to move slowly, Morgan slipped quietly toward the door.

Bob Gale had been watching the sling-armed man and the young troublemaker when a movement at the window caught his eye. Had it been of ordinary speed, some passerby on the boardwalk, it probably wouldn't have attracted his notice, especially with all that was happening inside. But the move's studied deliberateness, its stealth, alerted Gale and without even thinking he reached beneath the bar—just as the bat-wing doors burst open and the second of the pair stood in the doorway, his Colt in hand, aimed at the sling-armed man with the gun.

"Watch it!" Gale shouted, and raised the sawed-off above the bartop.

Morgan's finger had started to squeeze the trigger when the bartender's shout distracted him and, his eyes flicking, the mustached man suddenly saw the twin barrels of the 12-gauge trained on him. He found himself staring into the black mouths of a gun that at four yards would lift him off his feet. The barman's eyes were all-business and even if Morgan managed to redirect the pistol and squeeze off a shot, the shotgun's blast would still kill him. All this Morgan's brain registered in an instant, and he froze. But the sling-armed man had turned his eyes to him, and in that split second Rax was moving, grabbing at something on the bar, yanking his pistol from its holster and raising it toward the stranger. And Rax was fast: He got off a shot even as the sling-armed man crouched and fired. The two blasts overlapped, sounding a single, deafening report, and Rax folded as a bottle exploded over Clay's shoulder, glass fragments raining everywhere as a fine spray of whiskey scented the air; but the barkeep, with grimacing mouth, kept his big, white-rimmed eyes fixed on Morgan, and although Morgan's shoulders jerked with the sound and with their own need of movement, he dared not budge. Clay spun to face him, training his revolver: "Set it on the floor, Morgan—*now!*"

For another moment Morgan still didn't move. Then, looking at Clay with cold, flat eyes, and conscious also of the barkeep's scattergun, he opened his fingers and let the .44 clatter loudly to the floorboards.

"Who are you, mister?" he asked. "Seems to me I'd recollect if we met."

Clay moved to him quickly, keeping his gun

trained, and snatched up the fallen revolver. Grimly Clay said, "The name's Clay. You worked for Lardon. Now I'm takin' you back to Sharpton."

Morgan blinked. "*You're* fixin' to bring me back?"

"No others," said Clay.

"You *alone?*" Morgan said, and he wore a disbelieving smile. "Just you—like *that?*" He nodded at Clay's arm.

"Me is all it'll take," Clay said flatly. "We'll be leaving directly. I want to make good time."

Morgan eyed Clay slyly. "It's a long ride, pardner. You just might find you'll have your *hand* full." And with that he laughed long and loudly.

Chapter Twenty-three

The sun sat low on the horizon as the two riders made their way across the flats.

"What about water?" grunted Morgan, turning in his saddle.

"You just had some," said Clay, looking ahead at the man he had told to ride where Clay could watch him. "You can hold out 'til we make camp. I am."

"Gettin' sore wrists," Morgan complained.

Clay said nothing.

The sun slipped lower, its brightness softening until they could gaze at it, a gold dollar sitting on the horizon. In the distance the country gave way to hills, hinting at the steeper climbs ahead.

"All right," Clay said after a while. "This'll do."

Morgan drew the reins to his chest with both hands—both because between them hung a length of gleaming chain. The Bodie bartender had bought a six-foot length at Clay's request at Novak's hardware store, along with a pair of sturdy brass padlocks whose keys resided in Clay's shirt pocket. In the waning sunlight the chain flashed between Morgan's wrists but also along the remaining four feet trailing down the side of his saddle to disappear into his saddlebag. A muffled *ka-chink-a* had sounded with each step of the horse's plodding hooves.

"So what's your interest in all this anyways?"

They had finished plates of beans and hardtack and sat across the fire from one another. Morgan leaned against his saddle on the ground before the fire, a fork still in his hand. Clay leaned against his saddle as well, his dish beside him, the Colt resting balanced on his thigh.

"My interest?" Clay replied.

"In this here. Doin' this. Takin' me back," said the shackled man.

Clay sipped a cup of scalding coffee. "Let's say it seems the right thing," he said. "What's fair."

"Fair," Morgan repeated. "Fair for who?"

"Maybe not for you, but for the people the fire hurt."

Morgan was quiet a moment. " 'Cause I tell you, you got no call to be takin' me back—not for attempted murder."

"If you're gonna deny the whole thing, save it 'til we're back in Sharpton."

Morgan took a sip of coffee, eyeing Clay above the rim of the cup. "No," he said, lowering the drink. "No, I ain't denyin' I was there. You saw the brands, the spur wheel, the money. . . . Hey, I'd be dumb to say I wasn't there. But you got all wrong what happened—"

"A boy nearly died—might be dead by now," Clay said flatly. "A young fella might've died, an old man's barn burned an' some stock got wiped out in a fire set deliberate. Now which part have I got wrong?"

Morgan lowered the cup and his eyes got sharp. "Look, all right, we set it. But we was just followin' orders—"

"Followin' orders!" Clay snarled, and with a backhand motion flung the remainder of his coffee into the fire, making the flames hiss and sending a small cloud into the night sky.

"Look," Morgan said. "It's like this. It was supposed to be mostly just smoke. We was gonna light 'er then open the stalls right away, run out to our horses an' fire some shots to wake ever'body. It was just to scare 'im, see? So he'd sell. Lardon offered him a good price—"

"Good according to Lardon?" Clay asked sourly.

"Well, yeah—no! I mean . . ." Morgan shook his head. "Listen, good price, bad price—that's not what I'm gettin' at. It wasn't supposed to happen how it did. But the kid just come outta nowheres." Morgan set down his coffee and leaned toward Clay, his face flickering red and yellow across the flames. "Rax, he took a grab at the kid, they both fell, and the kid hit his head—got knocked cold. Then Rax headed for the door. I said wait, we couldn't just leave him, but

Rax pulled his gun. . . . You saw how fast he was. He said since the kid seen us, we had to leave 'im. I said no, but Rax had his gun up, an' I swear, he'd a killed me if I argued." Morgan looked at Clay earnestly. "On my mother's grave, all I meant was to scare the old man. Not for nobody to almost die—least of all some kid. You gotta believe me!"

Clay looked levelly at the other man. "Why is that?"

Morgan cocked his head and eyed Clay warily. "Why—? Why *what?*"

"Why do I got to believe you?"

Morgan's eyes widened in surprise. *"Why?"* His tone bordered on indignation. "Listen, what do you think they'll do to me if I go back? They don't know it was Rax—they'll hang me!"

"Tell the judge like you told me."

"No judge'll listen! Lardon'll say I'm a liar an' who do you think they'll believe—me, or him with all his money?"

"A man makes his own choices and pays the price."

"But does it seem right to you I should die for settin' a barn fire? You call *that* fair?!"

"I can't help you, Morgan. You shoulda thought a that before."

Morgan sat quietly a moment. Then his eyes grew sly. "Listen, Clay, you got close to $150 off Rax an' me there." He nodded toward the saddlebags at Clay's feet. "That's a healthy piece a change. Well, it's yours—take it! My horse an' gear, too! Just mount up, toss me the keys an' my canteen an' we'll call us square. Listen, what could be fairer than that?''

Clay shook his head. ''I didn't come after you for a horse and some money.''

''No? Well why are you doing this? 'Cause you're a nice fella? I don't believe in nice fellas. I think you got your own reasons. . . .''

Clay looked up sharply.

''Maybe,'' Morgan continued, ''it's *there*.'' He squinted at Clay's dead arm. ''You was born like that an' you're mad at the world.''

''I'd let that alone,'' Clay said.

''Yeah?'' Morgan eyed him closely. ''I'm right, ain't I? That's why you're so touchy.''

Clay's eyes hardened. ''You were better off not askin', but since you're so curious, no, you're wrong. It was more recent this happened. In fact, just three weeks ago—in a barn fire.''

Morgan stared. ''Wait, you're not sayin'. . . . Oh, gosh!''

''You ready to let it drop now?''

''All this talk about fair an' unfair. . . . Fair's got nothin' to do with it. You're after who done *that*!''

Clay rinsed the cup. ''That ain't the reason—not altogether.''

''Ha! An eye for an eye—that's what it's about! Don't tell me it ain't personal. . . . 'Justice,' 'fairness'—that's hogwash!''

''I ain't tryin' to convince you.'' Clay tossed another stick onto the fire. ''But if I only wanted revenge, don't you think I'd put a bullet in you by now?''

Morgan sat and chewed on that one a moment.

Clay nodded. "All right, now it's time to turn in."

"You figger on sleepin' with one eye open?" Morgan asked.

"I got a different idea." Clay slipped two fingers into his shirt pocket and tossed one of the keys to the manacled man; Morgan raised both hands to catch it, the sound of the chain sharp in the night.

"Go ahead, open one," Clay said.

Morgan hesitated, then quickly tried the padlock on his right wrist; he looked at Clay as he tried to twist the key, then frowned and fit the key into the other lock. This time the spring-loaded shackle snapped sharply open. Morgan rubbed his freed left wrist then held his palm out. "Okay, now the other. . . ."

Clay laughed shortly. "That's not what I had in mind." Drawing the Colt again, Clay held the revolver loosely at his side. "On your feet."

Morgan rose uncertainly.

"Step over by that dogwood," Clay said, gesturing with the sidearm.

Morgan did as ordered, moving to the edge of camp.

"Yeah?" he said. "Now what?"

"Run the free end there 'round the trunk, an' let's hear that lock snap," Clay said. "Then you tug 'er for me a couple times."

"Now hold on!"

"Do it, Morgan. Then I'll get your bedroll an' you can bunk down."

"What, locked to a tree!"

"You'll rest easier not spendin' the night figurin' ways to bushwhack me," Clay said. Grimly he smiled. "I'll rest easier, too."

Clay lay gazing at the stars. His prisoner lay across the fire a safe three or four yards' distance. Clay listened to the sounds of the night—crickets, the rustling of leaves. He accustomed himself to their loudness and range, knowing he would sleep through them as they sounded now, but would wake with any appreciable change. The chain clinked as the other man shifted position. There would be that sound, too—like that, but no louder.

What Morgan had said, Clay thought, unfortunately made some sense.

If in fact Morgan hadn't been directly responsible for the boy, then maybe it wasn't fair he might hang for Rax's crime. But who knew what really happened in the barn? Of the three people there that night, only Morgan could tell his story. Could a judge and jury determine the truth? Clay didn't know. And if they couldn't, could they administer justice? The legal system left much to be desired, the fact that it hadn't yet gotten Lardon proved that. But a man had to believe in justice *somewhere*. Those times Clay had thought there was none—immediately following the fire and, for that matter, after Rachel's death—he had been nearer despair than at any time in his life.

He had always been a man of action because he believed action made a difference. But if events could happen so randomly, and pain inflicted so unfairly, then did action have any point? Clay had just said fairness prompted him but had there been other reasons? If these men were responsible for Callie's pain, then he had a score to settle on her behalf. Morgan had said his score was personal and no doubt that figured in. And maybe Clay's guilt about young Danny? And to return the Cookes' kindness? And perhaps even to impress Callie? There seemed so many possible explanations for anything a man did, or tried or wanted to do, how could he ever claim to know his real reasons?

In any case, if the natural universe was unjust, it seemed all the more reason for people to affirm justice when they could.

One of the horses nickered. Clay listened a moment. When he felt satisfied it was nothing, he realized he'd been doing it again: Reflecting. Pondering. Yes, his time abed had changed him, maybe forever. But for better or worse, he wondered?

He sighed, and became aware he'd been cradling his right elbow with his good hand. Had he felt an ever-so-slight tingling at the fingertips? Not likely, he thought. Probably his exhaustion catching up with him, and his tired brain playing tricks on him.

He closed his eyes and slept.

Chapter Twenty-four

Leaning low, Clay blew a puff of air into the fire-pit. The white ash scattered to reveal a small bed of orange embers. With the sun barely up, the sky was still streaked with wide strokes of deep gray and a sliver of moon hung above. Clay set a fistful of match-size twigs loosely atop the glowing embers, filled his lungs with the chill morning air, and blew again, this time long and evenly. Wisps of gray smoke began to curl from the sticks, and when he stopped to inhale, the embers warmed his face. He blew another long breath and as he trailed off, the twigs flared suddenly into a small, fist-size fire, fingerlike flames flickering amid the twigs. The sight stirred Clay as it always did, after even the thousands of fires he had built through the years, sparking in him a satisfaction deep and primal.

He half turned. "Morgan, time to rise." He set slightly thicker sticks across the flame, enough to heat coffee, then turned and tossed one at the sleeping man, bouncing it off his leg. "Morgan."

In the gathering light the prone man grunted. The clinking noise sounded again, followed by Morgan's raspy voice as he swore. Morgan sat up, his hair awry, his free left hand rubbing his face, making the chain ring. "How's 'bout tossin' me a key so's I can relieve m'self?" Morgan pronounced the words coated with sarcasm.

Busy hanging the dented coffeepot from the wooden stake he had driven the night before, Clay didn't look up. "Back of the tree's fine," he said. "I don't wanna waste time fussin' with you an' those locks. Soon's we've had grub an' coffee we're headed out. We ride hard, we'll make Sharpton by early tomorrow."

Half an hour later, with the tin cups and plates packed, the sleeping rolls lashed tightly behind the cantles and all else attended to, Clay approached his prisoner. "Let's ride," he said, and tossed the other man a key. Clay stood with his hand resting on the butt of his holstered revolver.

Morgan, on one bent knee at the base of the tree, stuck the key into the padlock.

"You thought about what I said?" he asked.

Clay watched him and waited.

" 'Cause it still ain't too late," the prisoner continued. He twisted the key and the shackle snapped open.

"Too late?" Clay raised his eyebrows.

''To let me ride,'' said the crouched man, standing. His left hand free, he drew the chain toward him, its bright steel links disappearing around back of the tree like a snake. ''Rax was behind the worst of it an' with him gone, everything's even. Okay, sure, there's *that,*'' Morgan said, nodding at Clay's slinged arm. ''But hangin' me won't bring it back.''

Clay squinted. ''We see things different, Morgan. You asked why I'm doin' this. Well, it's got something to do with . . . order. Oh, not just law and order, more like . . . *consequences.* Life's unpredictable and in ways that's good, but if certain things happen certain others *ought* to happen. I believe that.'' Clay looked at the other man. ''Which is why you're goin' back.''

Morgan stared at him. ''If I go back, I could hang.'' His voice was flat.

''You don't know that for sure.''

''If I go back, I'll likely wind up a dead man.'' Morgan stood facing Clay. Holding the chain, his right hand seemed to weigh it. He dropped the lock in the dirt.

Clay stared at him. ''Pick it up.''

The other man didn't move.

''I'm tellin' you, Morgan, pick it up. You're goin' back. There's no question of 'if.' The only way you stay is dead.''

The other man continued to stare with hard eyes.

''Back in Sharpton,'' Clay continued, ''you got a chance. You'll get a lawyer. A trial.'' Clay scowled. ''Maybe it's more chance than I'd like. But here, you got none. Try somethin' here . . ." Clay shook his head and his hand remained on the pistol.

Morgan stood staring. Clay could almost see the thoughts running through his head. A six-foot chain . . . nearly half again that distance between them. . . . And Clay quick with the gun, as he'd already proved.

Suddenly Morgan shrugged and his mouth spread in a sour smile. "Just don't tell me it ain't personal. It's an eye for an eye is what it is. Well, I'd do the same. But don't give me that 'justice' or 'fairness' hogwash 'cause, hey, you ain't no better'n me 't a'll!"

He bent and picked up the lock.

Clay nodded toward the chain. "Like yesterday. Not too much there between your hands. Then toss the key in the dirt for me."

Morgan wrapped the chain around his free left hand. But then he fumbled the lock and it slipped from his fingers, dropping with a thud. "Dang," he muttered, and bent for it—using the moment to twist the links an extra half turn around his free wrist.

He straightened, snapped the lock on and bared his teeth in a mock smile. "Aw'right?"

The land changed as they rode. Reddish sandstone faded to grayish white, and flatland gave way to inclines which produced sheer, rocky precipices with drops of 15, 20, and 30 feet or more. As they plodded along, Morgan, knowing Clay could not see his hands, twisted the links back again and found he had a couple of links' play; he could slide the loop an inch, almost two, down toward the knuckles of his left hand. A while ago, complaining of hunger, he had persuaded Clay to give him a piece of jerky. Morgan had palmed part of it, and now he rubbed the greasy meat against the back of his hand and wrist. Slowly but doggedly he worked the loop bit by bit for the better part of an hour, until he sensed one last hard pull would do it. Coughing loudly, he leaned to one side to spit, and, using the motion to mask his action, he jerked the chain while clutching the lock with his right hand. His left hand came free. He kept it low beside the other. "How 'bout we stop for water?" he said, feeling the chain heavy in his hand. He half turned in his saddle and saw Clay shake his head.

"Not yet. We stop as much as yesterday, we'll never get there. No, you're good for a while longer."

They continued on. But soon after, adjacent to a precipice, Morgan suddenly stopped. Clay reined in behind him. "What's the matter?"

"Animal's limpin'."

Clay's eyes narrowed. "I didn't notice."

"Started back around that last bend. Just a little at first, but now worse. . . ." Morgan leaned sideways frowning down at the animal's right side.

"Walk 'im for me," Clay said.

Morgan prodded the roan with his heels and the animal stepped forward, but immediately Morgan reined in again. "See, there? No question. I can feel 'im favorin' his right foreleg. He must'a picked up a stone." Morgan looked back over his shoulder and grinned wryly. "We don't get it out, he'll go gimpy, then I'll have to ride with you."

"All right," Clay said. "Do like before—me first, you sit tight a minute." Wanting to be on the ground covering his prisoner as Morgan swung down, Clay dismounted. He let the Appaloosa's reins hang as he moved toward Morgan's animal.

"I just hope we got 'im in time," Morgan said, twisting in his saddle to see Clay touch his hand to his sidearm. "I hate to see a animal suffer." And with that Morgan suddenly drew the chain from the saddlebag, its full six feet extending and flashing in the sunlight, and whipped it around, slicing the air toward Clay's head. Clay saw Morgan's sun-flaked lips snarl above his yellowed teeth, saw the dark eyes flash and Morgan's neck cords bunch beneath his unshaved jaw, and Clay jerked his head back—but not in time to avoid the chain's stinging jolt, a heavy blow that opened a gash across his head. Then Morgan was diving off the horse, slamming Clay hard with his shoulder. Both went down, Clay taking the worst.

On his knees above his dazed captor, Morgan drew back his left fist and drove it from the shoulder at Clay's face, but Clay twisted away and Morgan's knuckles struck stone. He grunted and Clay lashed out his own fist, bracing himself with his boots against the rock beneath. Fist met jaw, but Morgan still was on top, and, scrabbling at Clay's gunbelt, he seized one of Clay's Colts. Clay backhanded the gun from the other's grasp, but now Morgan fell upon Clay with the chain between his fists, forcing the steel across Clay's throat, pressing with all his weight. Their faces inches apart, Clay felt the other man's breath in his nostrils and the cold, hard steel crushing his windpipe. Desperately he jammed his fingers beneath the links and lurched left then right, but to no avail. With his chest pounding, and knowing he must risk all, Clay jerked his hand free and drove its heel up hard against the other's jaw, snapping Morgan's head backward. Clay rolled hard to his left, the cliff-edge only inches to his right, but Morgan scrambled into a crouch and kicked at Clay, his boot tip finding the fallen man's ribs. Clay grunted and sensed himself at the very edge of the thirty-foot drop; Morgan's foot drew back again but suddenly Clay rolled toward the chasm, as much as he dared, empty space opening beneath his back. The other man's boot grazed his head, the pointed toe brushing past, and in that very instant that Morgan's boot met no resistance and he leaned slightly off-balance, Clay darted out his hand, snatched the glinting links, and yanked, jerking the chain across his body. He felt the other man's weight gently yield, and glimpsed Morgan's eyes, small and fierce one moment, wide with surprise the next, as he realized what was happening. Morgan's free hand clawed at the air so that he actually did hang there, at an impossible angle, for a long moment before suddenly plunging out of sight, shrieking, the chain jerking taut in Clay's hand and starting to drag him until he loosened his fingers and the links raced through them. Then there hung a moment of dead silence followed by a heavy *thump,* like a bale of hay dropped from a silo, and then the short, sharp, echoing ring of the chain striking rock. Then nothing, absolute silence.

* * *

Clay scrambled to his feet. Thirty feet below, Morgan lay on his back in the sun, one leg straight, the other bent at the knee, his hands flung wide with the silver chain pooled beneath his wrist. And even as Clay watched, the rock beneath the fallen man's head went suddenly a bright, shining red.

Clay dashed to his mount, snatching his canteen and slinging the cord over his head. He rushed ten or so yards down-trail to where the cliff sloped more gradually, and made his way down, loose rock crumbling and skittering beneath his boots as he half-slid down the perilous thirty-foot incline amid a cloud of dust.

Morgan lay as he had fallen and for just the briefest instant Clay paused: He had learned almost the hard way not to underestimate the other's wiliness. But Morgan's head lay in a pool of blood already dulling in the hot sun, and as Clay drew yet closer he saw a carmine line trickling from the fallen man's ear. *That's it, then,* Clay thought grimly. He set his lips and kneeled, pressing his ear to the other man's chest. A beat sounded faintly. Clay shifted to block the sun from Morgan's face.

"Morgan," Clay said. *"Morgan."* Clay tugged the bandanna from his pocket, bit out the canteen's cork, wet down the blue-checked cloth and set it across the fallen man's sweat-slick forehead. Morgan's breath caught audibly, and he winced.

"Morgan," Clay said again. "Can you hear me?"

The other man's eyes fluttered open.

"Dang," Morgan said through cracked lips. For a

moment his eyes blinked vacantly, then they focused on Clay. "Say, it's supposed to be you down here . . ." His lips twitched in what Clay knew was supposed to be a smile.

"You want water?" Clay asked.

The other shook his head slightly. "How bad—?"

Clay paused. "Not good."

Morgan sighed, which seemed to pain him. "Always thought I was too mean to die—guess I was wrong." Blood dribbled from the corner of his mouth.

"Listen, was it really Rax?" Clay asked.

Again Morgan's lips twitched. "No point lyin' now, eh? It was me." Morgan looked at Clay. "I give that a little fella in the barn credit: He had sand!" He sighed again. "Well, everybody dies sometime. . . . I guess I didn't expect to kick off in bed. But you know the worst of it?" He had to force the words. "That polecat Lardon gets off scot-free." Morgan grimaced, although whether from pain or bitterness, Clay could not tell. "He skunked us outta our money an' gets away with it. An' when he hears Rax an' me's gone, he'll prob'ly get a big laugh out of it! Man, I wish he was comin' with me now! I figured to settle with him sometime, but I guess now I'm gonna miss my chance. . . ."

Clay's eyes narrowed. "Listen, maybe you *still* got a chance."

Morgan looked at Clay.

"Sign a confession," Clay went on. "Say it was him put you up to it. . . . We can do it right here, right now. I'll write it, you sign. I got a pencil an' some paper in my saddlebags."

"It'll take more than a piece a paper to bring down Brack Lardon."

"I got more," Clay said, thinking of the spur wheel and kerosene can. "But a confession might make the difference that counts."

Morgan breathed with difficulty.

"Listen," Clay said, "Do it 'cause it's the right thing or to get back at him or for whatever reason you like—I don't care about which right now. I'm not tryin' to change your views at this point. Probably a lotta good gets done in this world for all kinds of reasons, and maybe it doesn't always matter what they are."

Morgan's eyes seemed to gaze into the distance. "I'll be dead, but I'll *still* bring him down." He smiled. "I like that."

Clay rose brusquely. "I'll be right back."

At the horses, he found a pencil stub with a broken point; no matter, he could sharpen it with the bowie. From the other saddlebag he brought a scrap of brown wrapping paper from the jerky. Quickly folding it, he jammed it inside his shirt. And then suddenly he felt it again. That tingling. He looked down at his fingers and saw them twitch. They *moved*. Was his arm coming back as the doc had said it might? Clay felt his heart jump. But this wasn't the time for celebration yet. He had a man waiting who might not be able to wait much longer.

"Hang tight, Morgan," he called, and again made his way down the slope.

Morgan lay as Clay had left him, his face turned toward the sun.

"You say it in your own words," Clay said, carefully making his way down the remaining few yards, loose stone crumbling beneath his boots. "I'll write it, then you sign 'er—" Clay stopped. A large, shining-green fly, bright as bottle glass in the sun, sprang up sharply from the fallen man's forehead, buzzed loudly in a quick, tight, angry corkscrew, then lighted again on Morgan's partially open mouth.

The fallen man never flinched.

Chapter Twenty-five

"Shank, I pay these men to work, not loaf. Keep an eye on 'em unloading—see they don't shirk!"

Brack Lardon, swinging down from his favorite cutback, watched the ranch wagon, piled high with supplies, rumble on past toward the barn. The sun beat down unmercifully, casting sharp shadows across the yard. "An' take my horse," the rancher added, handing his reins up to the mounted hired man.

Shank straightened in his saddle, none too gently spurred his mount, and led his employer's animal toward the barn.

Lardon turned toward the big house. Rides to town always left him hot and tired. By all rights he had no reason to make such trips, except his men were such idiots he knew they couldn't be trusted to accomplish anything otherwise.

As he strode toward the building, he noted two horses at the rail. The first, a sturdy Appaloosa, he had seen before, although he couldn't place it exactly. It gave him a strange twinge of uneasiness, though, which might have prompted him to study it further were he not distracted by the second animal—familiar for its B-over-L brand. Lardon realized as he drew closer that he also recognized the animal itself: Dirk Morgan's roan! So Morgan was back! Doubtless he had gambled away all his money and had come to ask for more. Well, if he thought he'd get another cent he was dead wrong. That the former ranch hand had even dared return enraged Lardon. And where was Morgan now? Could he possibly have gone into the house uninvited?

Stamping across the porch and through the door, Lardon stormed at full tilt down the hallway. As he neared the open study door he caught a familiar whiff that doubly incensed him as he realized that Morgan had helped himself to the rancher's humidor.

Bursting through the door, Lardon roared, "Morgan! What do you think you're—"

But the rancher froze in midstride and his words caught. For on the corner of the desk sat not his former ranch hand, but none other than the sling-armed man—Will Clay. The visitor's hat lay on the desk beside him and a cigar was between his teeth as he gazed at Lardon levelly.

"Glad you could make it," he said.

The rancher stared.

"I understand you bein' surprised," Clay continued. "Boose fouled up, didn't he?"

Lardon's face grew dark. He continued into the room, whipped off his hat and flung it aside. "I got no idea what you're talkin' 'bout! And where'd you get that roan?"

"Recognize it, do you? Yeah, it's Morgan's." Clay's manner was grim. "He's dead, Lardon. So's Rax. Boose, too."

The rancher stood staring. "I don't believe it—you're lyin'!"

"Oh, yeah, that's right—now I recollect. You're a big one for proof, aren't you? Well, like you say, it *is* Morgan's roan. An' in the saddlebags you'll find Boose's gunbelt an' Rax's spurs—the busted rowel and the matching other."

Lardon just stood there staring at Clay. For a moment he seemed at a total loss for words.

Clay looked hard at him. "Add up the rowel, kerosene can, an' the money I took off those men, plus the reason you had to burn Cooke out, an' it spells the makin's of a strong case against you, I'd say."

But the rancher spoke loudly. "Hey, some ol' spur wheel? A burnt tin can. . . . All circumstantial evidence! It won't hold up no more'n the last time you barged in here half-cocked!"

Clay slowly shook his head. "Fact is, I got somethin' more now."

The rancher raised his eyes.

"Before Morgan died," Clay said, "he confessed. Said it was you behind the fire, that you paid him and Rax."

The rancher's eyes glinted as he smiled. "Too bad he's dead, eh?"

Clay brought a folded piece of brown paper from his shirt pocket. He held it between his index and middle fingers for Lardon to see.

The rancher looked annoyed. "What's that?"

"Before he died he didn't only tell me everything, he agreed to sign a confession." Clay held up the piece of paper. "The signed confession of a dying man's likely to carry some weight with a jury, don't you think?"

Lardon frowned.

"Yep," Clay went on, "add it to the other evidence an' it might make all the difference in the world."

The rancher reached out his hand. "Here, let's see that—"

But Clay withdrew the slip and returned it to his pocket. "Plenty of time for that later, you'll probably have time to read it over and over, most likely. For now, I'd just as soon you didn't get your hands on it."

"Yeah? Well who says it's even Morgan's signature? You could of writ it yourself."

"The hotel register in Bodie's got his signature an' soon's I leave here I'm gonna wire Bodie's sheriff an' ask him to hold it as evidence in an arson and attempted murder case. Any judge with eyes will see they match."

Lardon ducked his head and looked at Clay from lowered brows. In a harsh whisper he croaked,

"Why—why are you doing this? You're not the law. You're not even the old man's kin!"

"A fair question," Clay grimly allowed. "An' one I been askin' myself." He shook his head. "Morgan thought it was just revenge, but for me it keeps comin' back to fairness. After the fire, I was at my lowest. What I thought was an accident left me like this. Lord knows things happen in this life that seem unfair, with about all we can hope for is the strength to carry on. But then when I realized there were people behind this—*you* were behind this—I knew I could do something about it." Clay shook his head. "But say, any talk of fairness an' duty . . . I got a feeling it's wasted breath on you, so I'll stop." He rose from the chair.

"Now wait a minute—where do you think you're going!"

"I got the law to see. . . ."

"Now hold it, Clay, just hold on! That letter . . . you leave it here."

"I don't think so—"

"Listen! Put it on the desk. I'll give you all the money you'll ever need."

"It's not for sale." Clay reached for his hat.

"All right, listen! Cooke can have his land back. I'll even give him some profit—a *small* profit, but a profit."

"Unless I'm mistaken, when the circuit judge sees this note, not only will you wind up behind bars but Floyd Cooke will get his land back an' somethin' extra in reparation." Clay moved toward the door.

"Clay!"

Ignoring the calls that followed him, Clay strode resolutely down the hallway.

Outside, he stepped to his horse. The door opened behind him and he heard Lardon shout again: "Clay!"

Several men nearby turned. A man ahorse beside the barn looked toward them. Clay recognized the man he'd seen earlier with Boose. The horseman started toward them.

"Clay, I'm tellin' you for the last time!" Lardon stepped off the porch.

Clay glanced around to confirm the rancher was unarmed, then reached for the reins at the rail.

"Well look who's back!" It was the horseman.

Clay turned to him. "Watch yourself," he said. He began to undo the reins.

Shank angled his horse so that Clay stood off to the horseman's right side. "Say, didn't you hear? You's bein' told to stay put."

"I don't take orders from thievin', lowlife polecats and any who try to give me some generally wind up sorry."

"Clay, it's your last chance!" shouted Lardon.

Clay and Shank eyed one another.

"Your boss burned Floyd Cooke's barn an' almost killed his grandson," Clay said. "Maybe you didn't know that before, but you know it now. I'm headed to the law. You can try to stop me—that's your privilege. But it may be the last mistake you make."

Shank's left hand held the reins steady as his right rested lightly on his thigh. He and Clay watched one another.

"You talk like you're fast," Shank said. "Are you? I mean, for a one-arm gimp."

"One hand is all it'd take to put a bullet through your heart," Clay said.

They regarded each other for some moments. The others watched silently. Then suddenly Shank's hand was moving—snatching the grip of his sidearm, jerking it free, the muzzle clearing leather—but an explosion sounded and Clay stood with his leveled Colt smoking. Shank crumpled, his pistol falling to the dirt, and then he toppled from the saddle, one foot twisting in the stirrup and the frightened horse threatening to bolt before one man moved quickly forward to grasp its bridle.

Lardon stood with eyes big. "You . . . you gunned 'im down in cold blood!"

"It was a fair shoot-out," Clay growled. "I warned 'im, but he drew on me anyway."

The rancher stepped forward. "You think you can outgun *all* these men?"

Clay looked grimly around at the dozen faces watching him, his eyes finally resting on the rancher. "I don't think I need to try." His voice deep, he spoke loudly enough for all to hear. "You've had some misfits working for you, Lardon, and maybe still have one or two. But unless I'm mistaken, most of the men I see here are basically decent, hard-working, and law-abiding." Clay peered closely at the faces. "No, I don't think these men are hired guns who'd try to stop me from goin' to the law for justice." Clay turned his back and undid his reins.

Lardon wheeled on his men. "Anyone who wants

to keep workin' for me, you stop 'im—stop 'im *now*!'' he sputtered.

The men exchanged uneasy glances but no one moved.

Clay turned again to the rancher. '' 'Course you can try yourself, Lardon. You're wearing no gun, but I'll wait for you to strap one on.''

Lardon stood in near apoplexy, his eyes almost bugging with fury, his face flushed deep purple.

''No,'' Clay said with a grimace, ''I didn't think so. . . .'' He turned, raised his boot to the stirrup, grasped the horn and began to swing up.

A scuffle of movement sounded, and someone shouted ''Watch 'im!'' Clay ducked as an explosion sounded and a slug whizzed past his ear; he twisted even as Lardon fired again from Shank's fallen pistol, but then Clay's own Colt was in hand. Spinning around, he shot.

Chapter Twenty-six

Clay spotted them as the Appaloosa crested the hill: two riders, one thin and hunched, the other also thin but sitting straight, under a too-big floppy hat. Clay's heart jumped. He squeezed his horse's ribs and broke into a gallop.

The other horsemen turned when they heard the Appaloosa's hooves.

"Floyd!" Clay shouted, *"Danny!"* Then he was reining in beside them, grateful for the welcome he read in their eyes.

"Clay," Floyd Cooke said. "You're back!"

Clay was shaking his head, grinning, looking from the boy to his grandfather. *"He's all right,"* Clay said, ducking his head toward the youngster.

"Come out of it the day after Callie showed us your note," Cooke said. "Lena says it's miracle. For once I'm not of a mind to argue. He woke up slow, which was good—it gave the doc the chance to come."

"How you feel?" Clay asked the boy, beaming.

The boy smiled. "All right. A mite tired. . . ."

"As if he ain't slept enough!" Cooked turned to Clay. "But what about you? Where you been?"

"There was business to tend to, Floyd. Sorry to leave sudden."

The old man peered at him, unsure whether to press.

Clay nodded and started the Appaloosa forward. The two other animals fell in beside him. "It's finished now, though. What are you doin' out here anyway?"

Cooke shrugged. "We'll be leavin' soon an' I figgered, well, to ride the land one last time with the boy." He squinted off. "To say good-bye."

Turning to the old man, Clay marked how haggard and weary he looked. He would need help. "I don't think you need to do that, Floyd—say good-bye, I mean. . . ."

Cooke looked at him.

Clay squinted toward the mountains. "On the trail yesterday a man died, and at the time it seemed the meanest trick life could play. But it got me thinkin'. In a world that often don't serve up justice, it falls on people's own shoulders to make it happen."

Clay drew the slip of paper from his pocket.

"What you got?" Cooke asked.

Clay fingered the slip, then handed it to the old man. Cooke unfolded it.

"Why, this is nothin'—it's blank!"

Clay squinted again at the distant peaks. "All the same, it wound up showing an awful lot about some men." He turned toward his two riding companions. "Come on, I'll tell you about it on the way back."

By the time they reached the shack it was nearly dark—just about the same time of evening, Clay realized, when he had first laid eyes on the settlement. Soft yellow light filled the windows and food smells hung in the air. In all, Clay couldn't have conjured a more inviting scene. He felt he wanted to say something, but wasn't sure what, nor even what his statement's form should be: An offer? A request? Maybe some combination of the two. But then the cabin door flew open and out burst Callie, running with streaming hair to meet him. And Clay felt that whatever phrase he chose, the words just wouldn't matter all that much.